WILDER

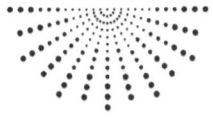

PAMELA JEFFS

four INK
PRESS

Cover design by Four Ink Press

Formatting by Four Ink Press

Language: Australian English

ISBN:

978-0-6453127-4-4 (pbk)

978-0-6453127-5-1 (ebk)

Visit www.fourinkpress.com

*Dedicated to the daughters of
difficult fathers.*

CHAPTER ONE

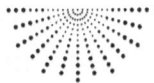

"We'll head straight to the police station," says Dad, "and you let me do the talking." My father's steely gaze remains fixed on the horizon. His fingers tremble on the steering wheel. An alcoholic's tell. I don't answer him; it's better not to when he's in a mood.

He glances at me and his lips twitch as if he's about to say something else but he doesn't. The knot of anxiety in my belly eases just a bit. I'm thankful for his silence.

Outside, the grey day flicks past. It's the kind of grey that announces seasonal change, the time when the wind grows cold and crisp with a bite of ice to it—a breeze hailing from Antarctica. Autumn is quick in these parts to release her grip to winter.

Mount Field National Park glides by on the left. This portion of old-growth forest saved from logging, hunkers beneath the dark sky. Random droplets of rain begin to fall, splattering and spreading across the windscreen. The wipers squeak as they smear them away.

I hunch my shoulders and roll up the passenger window. At my touch, the heater blares. Warmth floods the Landcruiser's cabin but my toes are still cold, and there are months of worse to come. God, I hate winter in the south. Tasmania. End of the World.

Not that I can go anywhere else.

Not with my dad, Emmett, sick like he is.

Last time I left home he tried to kill himself. Off at university, I'm not sure what made me come home that exact weekend to visit. But when I did, I'd found him in the barn. Alone I had cut the rope and lowered him to ground. I don't know how he was still breathing.

Now I'm stuck. Sometimes pitied by the townsfolk, I've typically been branded as a weirdo—the girl without a future. Sometimes I pass mothers of old school friends in the supermarket and they whisper behind my back—

"Look, Joan, it's that poor girl, Reeva. To think she lives out there all alone with that monster who calls himself her father."

"Oh hush, Tanya. Emmett was a good man once. You know that."

"Do I? He murdered her mother, you know. Just a few days after Reeva was born!"

"There was never any proof of that."

The township of Maydena appears over a crest. Small, it's just a speck on the snaking length of Gordon River Road. Framed by the verdant backdrop of national forest, the houses all sit low on their plots. A mix of faded weatherboard dwellings with their paint skins peeling, moss-stained bricks and older heritage sandstone. But they are sturdy enough, tough like the people living in them.

The scent of wood smoke sneaks past the old door rubbers and into the car. With the coming of the colder weather, the residents of Maydena have started to stoke their fireplaces. Hearths sitting cold and dead for the summer months are now cleaned and readied for the coming frosts. Newborn plumes of smoke rise from the chimneys, smearing a light grey patina against the darker sky.

The police station is a clean and well-maintained building. Single-storey, painted white and with an enclosed verandah, it hugs the corner of Junee Road and West Street.

A cruiser waits in the driveway. Dad eases in behind the vehicle, blocking it. A shadow passes by the office window, a brief flash of square-ended fingers pulling aside the blinds then disappearing.

The door to the foyer swings on well-oiled hinges. Dad steps across the threshold; his bulky frame fills the room like a stallion in a stall. Inside, the building smells like stationery. Like clean white paper. It gives the place a sense of being officious and important, even though it's much smaller than the station in nearby Bushy Park.

Constable Galen Mayer, with his green eyes and white-blond hair, stands behind the reception counter.

He hasn't aged since we were at high school together, always with the face of a boy. He was four grades ahead of me and several tiers higher in popularity. Everyone had a crush on him. Even me. Not that I ever said anything.

I suspect he knew though.

He always made a point of saying hello.

Today he looks as handsome as always, in a pressed uniform. He smiles at me.

I blush.

Dad scowls.

"Emmett. Reeva," says Galen, still smiling. "What brings you folks in today?"

"Where's Sergeant Williams?" growls Dad.

I just want to die with embarrassment. Why can't my father ever be pleasant?

The constable leans against the counter, cool and collected. "John is out this morning. I'm happy to help you though."

Dad sniffs. "Bloody horse thieves have hit our place."

Galen's forehead creases. "How many gone?"

"Just one." My father scratches his ear with finger-bitten nails. "They knew quality when they saw her."

"Echo, then?" asks Galen.

"Yup," replies Dad.

Echo. Our only thoroughbred. The rest of our horses are Shetland ponies.

"You sure the mare didn't escape?" Galen points towards the window and the forest beyond it. "The reserve is a pretty big place. She could be anywhere in there."

Dad runs a hand through his salt-and-pepper hair. The muscles in his cheeks bunch, a sure sign he's getting frustrated. My stomach constricts. I silently beg the constable not to push my father's buttons.

"I'm not an idiot, Mayer," says Dad. "The lock to her stall was broken and her bridle was missing. Someone walked her out."

Galen frowns. "Well, it seems you aren't the only one. All the horses were taken from the Anderson place last night too. That's where the sergeant is now."

The Andersons. I smirk. Couldn't happen to a nicer family. Their thoroughbred stud borders our farm, Tarina, and they often break the boundary fences to let their stock graze on our lush rear paddocks.

"ALL of their horses?" says Dad, eyebrows rising. "That's a lot of animals."

Galen nods. "Yep. Fifty, in fact. They woke this morning and their stables were empty."

"Suppose they blamed me for it."

"Your name was mentioned."

No love is lost between Dan Anderson and Emmett Castor. Especially since it was Dan who, all those years ago, first spread the rumours about my father murdering my mother—said he'd seen Dad in the forest that night with an axe.

"I haven't been anywhere near their place," says Dad.

"We know that. And you've done the right thing by

staying away," says Galen, no doubt recalling the last time Dad spoke to Dan in the local pub about ruining fences. A 'talk' that ended in bruised egos and broken teeth. "I'll call John and ask him to head out to your place and take a look around. He should be there by the time you get home."

Dad frowns, his grey eyes darken. Then he nods.

"Right-o," he says. "I'll expect to see him in a bit."

CHAPTER TWO

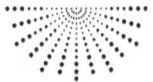

The sky breaks, the rain cutting rivulets in the dusty windscreen. Dad eases his foot onto the brake. The Landcruiser slows, its 4WD tyres biting into the wet, unsealed road. I lean closer to the window. The tall trees along the road toss their heads, wild against the storm. It's the rugged north boundary to the Anderson farm. We're close to home.

"Can't see anything in this damned muck," snarls my father.

He slams his palm on the gearstick and shifts down to third. The engine groans. I keep my attention focused outside on the dark forest that lines the verge —predatory, primordial. Beautiful. I swear there's something magic about those trees. I've always felt the draw of it—that attraction which informed my choice to study environmental science at university. I guess I wanted to help preserve these wild places.

I glance at Dad. That'll never happen now.

Lightning bristles across the sky.

I blink. In the afterglow, a shadow, fluid and quick, moves along the treeline to my left. I brush my fingers at the condensation on the glass. Another flash and the forest illuminates again. A silhouette, punch-cut black, stands out against the light. Long legs and arms. Smooth head. Claws.

Then it's gone, lost again to the shifting gloom and slicing rain. A chill tracks along my spine. Just a trick of the light.

"There she is!" Dad yells, his voice too loud in the cabin.

"Holy hell! Who?"

"Echo!"

My heart leaps. I peer out the windscreen. An after-image of the clawed shadow still lingers but there are no monsters this time, only Echo. The grey mare races ahead of us, eyes rolling and bridle dangling. Her coat clings to her, wet-slicked to darkness.

Dad punches the accelerator.

The ute slides, mud fans across the side window.

"It's too slippery," I say. "Let her go. We'll get her in the morning."

Another gear change. My father floors it. The Landcruiser heaves forward, engine growling as it strains to match the mare's speed. I grip the seat. Dad's eyes slew left, wild as the night.

"Dammit, Dad! Stop!"

He shakes his head. A single sharp jerk. His focus never leaves Echo. "She's too important. Can't leave her here to get hurt."

"Slow down. You're gonna kill us!"

Dad bares his teeth. "Don't be so bloody dramatic."

We sheer sideways. I grab the door handle and brace my feet.

The tyres slip on the waterlogged, clay-mud road. Dad curses and oversteers, his thick farmer hands, two vices crushing the steering wheel. Left, he turns, right and back left. The world spins.

Trees. Road. Trees. Road.

The *whip-crack* of breaking glass, a bite of pain in my arm, and my head hits the dash.

I wake with a start. Droplets of water, leaking in through the broken side window hit my cheek; tiny, cold slaps. I groan. Everything hurts. Rain drums a steady cadence on the roof and a dim, flickering light leaks in through the side window. I squeeze my eyes shut then open them. My vision clears. It's the indicator blinking. The glow fractures off the rippled surface of the shattered windscreen.

I wriggle but I'm pinned to my seat. The dash has crumpled forward and holds my legs prisoner. My left forearm stings too. I hiss at the jagged cut etched on the inner side from wrist to elbow.

Dad is unconscious. Still buckled in his seatbelt, he faces me, head resting against the steering wheel. His mouth hangs open, skin waxen in the orange glow of the flashing light. Blood runs from a cut on his forehead and seeps into his collar.

Is he dead?

I swallow and hold two fingers to his throat. Nothing. My breath hitches and I press harder. Still nothing.

"Dad," I whimper. "Please don't do this to me."

My hand trembles with more than just the cold. I count to three. Then six. I change position and then find his pulse. The breath I'm holding shudders out. I should have known better. My father is old-school Tasmanian—tough as Huon pine—it'd take more than a car crash to outright kill him.

But he's hurt. My stomach knots and for an instant I recall when I last saw him injured—an afternoon, not so long ago, in the barn. No. He's not going anywhere. Not here and not tonight. Not while I can save him.

Outside the car, moonlight has found a rent in the shredded cloud cover, painting the water-slick trees in silver light. The rain has eased and afternoon has fled into evening. We've been out of it for a few hours at least.

I jiggle my seat belt clasp and it clicks free. I press both palms against the dash and push. I'm wiry, but unusually strong—always have been. The panel groans and soon gives. The windscreen above buckles away with a crash. Outside, the car's bonnet, all crumpled like wet paper, is wrapped around a huge, rugged tree trunk.

I realise how lucky we are to be alive.

CHAPTER THREE

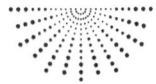

The car door opens with a tortured screech. I tumble to the wet ground, roll to my knees and brush the litter from my palms. I tug my mobile out of my pocket. The screen is smashed. No calling for help. Anxiety curdles my stomach. I need options.

Maybe I can make it to the Anderson farm. It's close, only about three kilometres from here. I glance at Dad and dismiss the idea as quickly as it formed. Easy isn't always right, especially when it comes to my father. He'll kill me if I go there for help. And I can't carry Dad out. He's over a hundred kilos. Even as strong as I am, hauling him as dead weight won't fly. I run a shaking hand down my ponytail. What do I do?

The distant rumble of an engine and the crunching bite of tyres on the water-slick road cut through the night. Headlights, beam on full, illuminate the trees in a sudden burst. Someone's coming.

Desperate, I race for the road, wet ferns tangling against my legs. I reach the verge just as Sergeant John

Williams's police cruiser roars past, heading back towards town. I sob, waving hands and yelling, but the old man's attention is fixed forward. I curse as the car disappears around a slight bend, gone as quickly as it appeared.

I stand on the road, head pounding and wrist burning, breathing hard.

"Damn it!" I scream.

A savage scream answers back.

My lungs tighten. Fear prickles along my spine.

I sense eyes on me.

Get back to Dad.

Anxiety nips my heels as I sprint back towards the car. Another blood-curdling scream tears past me, followed by the distant crack of breaking timber. I slide to a halt by the driver's side of the car. The door handle is ice against my palm but, undamaged, it opens easily. I unclip Dad's seat belt. He slumps sideways, moaning as his bulky frame presses precariously against the pillar. I almost faint with relief. Lucid, maybe he can walk himself out of here.

"Dad?"

"Reeva?" he slurs.

"We gotta go."

He nods.

Another stick cracks, closer this time. I glance over my shoulder. A small azure kingfisher sits on a nearby branch, staring back.

Dad's gaze flicks up. "Is it Echo?"

He's still worried about the damn horse. "No. Something else is out there."

I drag Dad upright. He pauses, chin tucked to his chest and shoulder braced against the door pillar.

"I just need a minute," he says, swaying.

I chafe at the delay but say nothing.

"Bloody hell," he says, pressing a hand to his temple. "I'm sorry about this, kid."

He must have hit his head pretty hard. My father never apologises.

"Don't worry about it," I say. "Let's just get home."

He tips his chin towards my arm. "You're hurt too."

"I'll be okay."

A third scream, closer this time, cuts through the night. Dad straightens, suddenly alert.

"C'mon Dad, we really need to go."

He grabs my wrist. "How far are we from home?"

I wince at his iron grip. "We're on Anderson's front boundary to the road."

Dad scans the night, his intensity frightening. "Wild Changers," he whispers almost to himself."

"What?"

Another scream.

His gaze locks to mine, then slips. He's groggy. "There's no time. Leave me here. Run for home. Don't look back."

My chance to protest is drowned by the noise of tearing vegetation. Foliage trembles. The edges of the plants blur and coalesce into something else—distorted images only half-formed. Bald heads give way to the hint of long limbs, teeth and claws.

It's the creature I saw before the crash, only there are more of them now.

The things leap through the undergrowth, movements liquid and the shape of their bodies in constant flux.

Terror overwhelms me, primal in its strength. "What are they?"

My father's voice cracks. "Changers. Now run and don't let 'em bite you!"

"Dad?"

His lips part into a grimace. "They can smell your blood. They won't stop. But I'll slow them up and give you a chance."

"What?"

"Go! I won't tell you again!"

A tone I recognise and it's the one I dread. It's his 'about to lose my shit' tone. My heart knots. I love my dad but I'm afraid of him too. That fear sends me sprinting away without another word. Maybe I can make the Anderson homestead.

Behind me, Dad swears.

Angry, unearthly chitters reply.

The forest plucks at me as I careen away. Self-recrimination for leaving my father behind all but cripples me. I sob against the tightness in my chest. I did the right thing. I did what he asked. I'll get help.

The noises fade. I push deeper through clusters of giant ferns and swerve around great moss-covered boulders. Sticks catch at my jeans and my boots slip in the detritus-littered forest floor.

The trees thin ahead. Hoping for an open paddock to gain some distance, I instead stagger into a small clearing that smells of mud, fresh cut lemon myrtle and eucalyptus.

I stumble to a halt, lungs and legs both burning. The glade is a scar in the bush, an open space strewn with woodchips and freshly hewn logs tumbled about like toothpicks; old-growth forest timber that most certainly would have been listed as protected. The stumps left behind, still skirted by ragged, flaking bark, glare naked to the night.

A fleeting thought—*Loggers?*

Snarls reverberate through the trees. The dense bush on the other side of the clearing beckons. I manage three steps more and I realise I haven't the strength to keep going. But I'm father's daughter— stubborn and resilient. I won't fall here without a fight. I gather myself and turn.

A small flash of blue and white catches my attention. The azure kingfisher again. It flits past me, low to the ground. With a sharp lift of wings, it rises and lands on the furthest stump.

"Follow me," it chirrups. "Hurry!"

Did the bird just talk?

The first changer breaks into the clearing with a shriek. The moonlight reveals its lean, blue-skinned humanoid form, purple lips and sharp canine teeth. Its almost-white eyes gleam.

All thoughts of birds flee. The strange creature stops, its throat rippling with a growl. Then it launches, teeth bared and claws slewing up clumps of earth as it streaks towards me. My stomach turns to liquid, fear tasting like metal on the back of my tongue. I squeeze my fists tight and the injury on my arm jolts, painfully.

The creature barrels into me with the force of a hammer. I grunt as we hit the mud and roll. I jab my forearm against the changer's throat. Its sharp animal teeth snap, inches from my nose; its pepper-ash breath all encompassing.

I blink away sudden tears as I'm elbowed in the nose. Mud smears into my eyes. Half-blinded, I see a human-shaped silhouette step in between myself and my attacker.

Dad?

The weight on my chest disappears as my attacker is flung off me like a rag doll. It lies sprawled on the ground, a metre away.

"Freedom is yours. Go!" snarls my defender. A male, but it's not Dad's voice.

"You would protect one of *them*?" growls the changer.

"Just this one."

The creature screams, the unholy noise raising the hair on my arms. Then it scrambles and flees into the forest.

"Thank you," I sob, wiping the mud from my face. I look up to find no one there.

Only the kingfisher hovering mid-air.

"You're still in danger," it trills. "They'll kill you if they catch you. Come with me."

The bird flits away, heading for a tall, hoary gumtree at the edge of the clearing. A small ring on its leg glows gold and the tree trembles. The trunk, one section scarred by old, greyed-out axe cuts, glows white then splits to create a tall, thin entrance leading down into the roots and earth.

"What the hell?"

"Stay or follow?" asks the bird. "Decide quickly."

Other screams filter out from the forest.

Dad …

I can't help my father if I'm dead. So, the bird and a magic doorway it is.

CHAPTER FOUR

A stone slide leads down into shadow. I quickly position myself on the edge and push off. The decline, glass-smooth, carries me with a helter-skelter pace both terrifying and exhilarating. In moments, I land with a hard, unexpected jolt.

It's dark and silent. I blink, but I may as well be blind. Claustrophobia presses and the anguish of leaving my father behind doubles in the absence of light. Guilt sweeps through me and suddenly I'm not sure if I have made the right choice. Those things outside have captured Dad for sure. I swallow. Past experience has proven that bad things happen when I'm not around to look after my father.

Anxiety swells, crowding the back of my throat. I need to go back.

"Bird?" I whisper. "Are you there?"

I reach across the uneven floor. To each side of me is empty space.

A brush of wings against my cheek.

"I am Havander."

I reach out again to emptiness. "I can't see anything, Havander."

"We are underground. You're safe here."

"We are buried underground?" I squeak, my voice a notch higher than I'd planned.

"Not buried. I'll strike the light, but please don't panic when you see me."

"Why would I panic?"

"Because it would be understandable if you did."

I bite my lip, forcing calm. A small blue spark ignites in mid-air and the room brightens—a large circular space with walls of smooth tree roots woven together like a basket.

The light expands and against it, for a moment, hovers the ephemeral outline of the kingfisher. The bird's wings extend and its body ripples—lengthens and solidifies—into something *else*. The brightness condenses into a heart-shaped orb centred on Havander's new body.

I scuttle backwards, fingers clawing at the floor. What have I just seen?

Don't panic, indeed …

Havander crouches on the floor, no longer a bird but humanoid in shape. His chest, visible through the opening of the grey robe he wears, is illuminated, or more like his heart, is beating bright behind a wall of mottled, blue and white, translucent skin. His head is bowed, the pate bald and smooth. He lifts his chin and his eyes find mine, their irises almost-white, the pupils, black.

Changer.

My breath hitches, adrenaline surges again. I keep my poise but teeter, uncertain which instinct to embrace—fight or fly.

Havander's gaze drops back to the floor. His whole manner screams submission as if to say—*you are safe.*

He carries no weapon, only the anklet on his leg, now grown in scale and formed of four interlocking rings.

Am I safe?

"Please," he whispers. "There's no need to fear me. Freedom is yours."

Those words, as spoken earlier. Realisation dawns. This is the man who stood between me and the changer outside.

I release a shuddering breath.

"But you are one of those ... *things.*"

"Yes, but unlike those topside, I won't hurt you."

"Why should I trust you?"

Havander slowly gets to his feet. Tall and thin, he towers over me. But standing, he also seems less like an animal.

"Because," he says, "I could have left you in the forest."

He makes a good point.

"Let me prove my sincerity." He gestures towards my injury.

I hesitate.

"Please," he says.

Fearless, I think to myself. *At least pretend to be fearless, Reeva ...*

The changer gathers my wrist into his hand. His long fingers trace the ragged tear in my flesh.

I wince and try to pull away but his grip tightens.

"This won't hurt," he says.

The light in his chest pulses and brightens. It travels through his limbs to gather in his fingertips. My injury absorbs the glow. Heat floods through me. My breath catches as the edges of the wound tighten and gather together. Flesh knits leaving a raised scar. Below the seam of tissue, my blood tingles. Then the rest of my body embraces the healing effect also, bruises and pulled muscles all settling to become whole again.

I brush my arm.

"You fixed it?" I say, breathless.

"Yes," he gasps, voice ragged.

Havander's chest heaves. On the inside of his arm, a faint red welt marks his skin as if he has somehow absorbed the injury. I don't like seeing it there, as if he has taken on my pain.

"Are you okay?"

"I just need rest. Healing depletes my energy."

He *healed* me, yet even though the act is irrefutable, I struggle to believe how it can be so. I clench my fist and windmill my arm, enjoying how it feels.

"Thank you," I say.

Havander nods.

Maybe it's okay to trust him, just for now.

"I need to get back," I say. "I was in a car accident before those changers found me. My dad is still out there, and he's injured."

"The other human was your father?" Havander

stumbles backwards to lean against the wall, shoulders slumped.

"Yeah."

"I understand, but I can't take you back myself though." He points to the anklet he wears. "This prevents me from going topside without approval. We need to speak with my keeper first."

"Your keeper?"

Havander's smile fades. "Yes. This is a control anklet. I'm a slave."

Even spoken as softly as they are, the changer's words hold challenge. I'll wager he doesn't consider himself someone's property.

I'm not about to argue with him. "Okay then," I say. "I'll follow you." I wipe my hand down my pants and extend it forward. "My name is Reeva, by the way. Reeva Castor."

Havander accepts the handshake, his skin cool against mine.

"Castor?" he asks.

"Yes."

"Your father's last name is Castor too?"

"Yes. He's Emmett Castor."

Havander nods as if some unspoken thought has been confirmed. He releases my hand and, seeming to have regained his strength, presses the largest tree root in the wall. The corded timbers shiver and slither apart to reveal a doorway.

"Let's get you back to him, Reeva," he says.

～

The view beyond the exit is unexpected. Stepping out onto the crest of a grass-covered hill we overlook a verdant underground world—a valley that meanders north for several kilometres before dissolving into darkness. I reel, taking in the lay of the cavern system. Monolithic stalagmites and stalactites dot the vista, their elegant, tapered forms framing the snaking lines of a thin, dark subterranean river at the valley floor. The watercourse is lined with ferns and trees critically endangered in the upper world. I recognise some of them from my brief studies at university—Juniper Wattle, Stuart's Heath, and Morrisbys Gum.

Overhead, large fireballs intermittently light the craggy ceiling of rock. The flaming orbs, contained and smokeless, hover like a flotilla of small suns. Their warm red-yellow glow illuminates all—the river, and in the near distance, a mid-sized settlement over which towers a white citadel. The opposite bank, only a kilometre or so away, holds vegetation-clogged ruins and a mouldering stone bridge that hunkers against dense forest.

"The Styx," says Havander. "Named long ago by a shipwrecked mariner who found his way to our world. When he saw this valley, he believed it to be the boundary between Earth and the deep Underworld."

"Styx? He must have been Greek."

"He was."

A quiet rustle sounds out behind us. I turn to see the roots framing the door slither together of their own accord. With the entrance gone, the sensation of being trapped closes around me.

"Hey! Where did the opening just go?" I ask.

Havander touches the now seamless column of roots stretching upward to the cavern's ceiling.

"The Elder Tree has closed the way," he says. "Its root system guards one of the gates between this world and that above."

I look up and recall the logged trees in the meadow above.

"What happens if those loggers come back and cut the tree down?"

Havander frowns. "There are two Elder Trees leading to this valley and they are guarded, but if they *were* to fall, we would be trapped here."

"We couldn't dig our way out?" I ask.

"No," replies Havander. "Only the root systems provide the doorways."

The cavern roof, even as high as it is, presses on me and my palms grow sweaty.

Havander points to the base of the hill. Grey stone ruins lay tumbled among the foliage there also.

"Down there is Live Well," he says. "My wilder keeper returned not long ago to secure a horse. I am to meet him there. He can grant you exit topside."

"Hang on," I say. "You guys have been stealing the horses?"

"The horses offered themselves freely to the wilders," replies Havander.

"Offered themselves?"

"They came willingly when asked."

Of course they did. Horses will follow anyone with a carrot.

"I need to have a serious chat with this keeper of yours. What did you call him? Wilder?"

Havander folds his hands together. "No. His name is Dacien. He is a wilder, as in 'not a human.'"

"And when you say not human ...?"

Havander chuckles. "He looks human but his kind are sometimes known as elementals."

"You can't mean as in fairy tales ... fire, earth, air, and water kind of people?"

"Don't forget those of aether," says Havander, serious. "They're just as important but are often forgotten in those stories."

CHAPTER FIVE

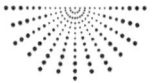

Havander's robes flutter as he strides down the slope. He looks at ease as his long hands swing loose. I consider what I've seen—what he can do. I'd like to think the changer is just a product of random evolution, but truth is, I can't consolidate the logic. The glowing, the healing, the shapeshifting—it can only be some kind of magic. Maybe fairy tales do hold the seeds of truth.

We push through a copse of Blackheart Sassafras and into a clearing at the base of the hill. Some kind of amphitheatre, or what's left of one, with broken seats and stepped terraces, lies half hidden by the vegetation. In the centre of the ruined arena, stands a half-sunken well, its sides curtained with moss and lichen. A teenage boy, looking just a few years younger than myself, lounges against it. His long charcoal jacket and pants are well tailored. Tall black boots cup his calves. The entire outfit has a strange sheen to it, like water rippling in sunlight. I've never seen anything like it before.

This must be Dacien.

Havander's keeper is good looking; I'll give him that. Something about his kind of prettiness reminds me a little of Galen Mayer—all fine features, full lips and cheekbones a girl would kill for.

But unlike Galen, something about this boy is certainly non-human. He looks normal, his stance casual, but there's a sense of leashed power about him, like a waterfall caged behind glass.

Is he magic too?

The thought flees. Dacien is holding something I recognise—a mustard-coloured bridle with *Tarina* embroidered on the strap.

I clench my jaw. "That belongs to my horse," I growl, pointing.

Dacien's eyes thin, storm-blue against the jet-black fall of his fringe. He juggles the bridle. On his wrist, a silver bracelet, crafted of interlocking rings like Havander's anklet, gleams.

"What's this, Havander?" the boy asks, ignoring me completely. "Humans are forbidden."

The changer bows his head, a gesture of submission subtly underpinned by his checked challenge. The way Havander defers to someone so young makes my skin crawl. It's not right.

"My apologies, Dacien," says Havander. "But the escapees were hunting Reeva. I was unable to secure her companion, but thought it prudent to rescue her. No need to give the others fuel to aid their cause."

A tiny line appears on Dacien's forehead. "The council won't like this."

Havander shrugs. "Surely there's no need to alert them. The forest will be clear by now. Grant me permission for access and I will return her topside."

Dacien rubs his chin. "The councillors will want to know she's been here."

Havander's shoulders slump. He seems unhappy but remains silent. I get the impression his preference would be to avoid their council at all costs.

The boy finally turns to me. "Your companion, a human also?"

I've never heard the word 'human' spoken before as if it were a disease.

Hello to you too, you arrogant little sod.

"Yes. I need to get back to find him."

"I see."

"I won't say anything to anyone about what I've seen here."

"Of course, you can't. Your people would think you are crazy."

Entitled brats are nothing new to me, but this guy takes the cake.

"So why is there a problem?" I ask. "Just let me leave."

Dacien's right eyebrow lifts. "Your companion is lost. He's effectively a prisoner of war. You can't help him."

"He is my father and he has a name. Emmett Castor. He's still out there, in danger, pretty much because you stole our horse from us. You can't expect me to leave him."

Dacien's eyebrow lowers, the planes of his face smooth into glacial stillness.

"Your problems are not my priority."

This boy's condescension pushes all my buttons. "You better make them your priority."

A hand settles, feather-like, on my shoulder. Havander gives me a slight squeeze.

A warning?

"Fine. Get me to your council then," I snap. "I'll get them to let me out."

The boy frowns. "If the changers have him, he's no longer the man you knew."

Dad's words ... *don't let them bite you* ...

I clench my jaw. "You have no idea how tough he is."

"We don't," says Havander, his voice calm, "but he is in terrible danger. Speak with the council as Dacien suggests. Ask them for help. They may choose to lend you aid."

"Or choose not to," adds Dacien.

My temper flares again and I glare at him. The young wilder returns the look, his presence dripping with disdain.

I straighten my shoulders. "Let's go."

"Not with you dressed like that, we're not," he replies.

I glance down. I'm filthy, clothes stained with mud and blood.

I brush at the marks on my shirt. "I don't care how I look."

"Perhaps not," says Dacien, "but you should care what the councillors think. So, unless you're a changer and can make new clothes out of your own skin, come closer."

Clothes from my own skin? Gross.

"I'm fine standing here, thanks."

"Come closer!"

"No. How are you going to sort new clothes anyway, hotshot?"

Dacien sniffs in frustration. Then he reaches across the well's opening and turns his palm upward. Threads of silver light coalesce in his hand. The strands build until they spill into the well. Twisting as if in a current, the light draws the water upward. A column rises past the stone rim, higher and higher until it breaks free. It hovers in the air, a clear, glistening and malleable bauble, suspended.

He flicks his wrist and sends the sphere of fluid spinning.

Awed, I clutch my forearms.

The boy stretches his fingers wide. The sphere splits, then splits again. Each piece reshapes, forming into sheets of glistening blue fabric. Dacien's magic imbues it, flashing like silver through the weave. His wrist twists and so does the material, curling and forming to become a simple, long sleeved, narrow-waisted dress that shimmers in the same way Dacien's clothes do. Another portion shears off the hem and tears into two. These sections thicken to form slim boots of a darker blue.

His work sinks to rest on the moss-covered edge of

the well. "New garments," says Dacien. "Get changed and we'll go."

"But it's a dress," I say.

"Yes. Is there something wrong with it?"

"I'm more a T-shirt and jeans kind of girl. You really expect me to wear a dress?"

Havander coughs again. I roll my eyes.

"Fine. Thank you." I snatch the frock and marvel grudgingly at the strange material; at how it feels both thick and thin at the same time.

I hold the garment up and raise my eyebrows sarcastically. "Don't mind me. I'll just find a tree fern to change behind."

CHAPTER SIX

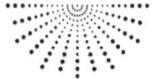

I wouldn't have picked them, but the dress and boots are comfortable. I relish the slither of the fabric across my shoulders as I follow Dacien along a well-worn path through the primordial forest.

As worried as I am about Dad, I can't help but appreciate this underground world. The atmosphere in the valley is sharp and clear—much cleaner than above ground. To the side of the path, heavy ferns drape across the moist ground, sweeping at carpets of dew-soaked moss and delicate grasses. A shadow slithers through the vegetation and I glimpse tawny fur, striped black. I've only ever seen a Tasmania Tiger in photos.

"She's one of the many animals that have taken sanctuary here," says Havander, as if reading my thoughts.

"It's a shame they have to hide. The world above is less for their loss."

Havander touches a wet fern leaf. He rubs the moisture between his thumb and forefinger. "Your race is still young." He wipes his fingers on his sleeve. "With time you can change to become kinder, then perhaps such creatures can return."

Dacien scoffs. "Change isn't the answer. Humanity will always embrace brutality. Just look at the course of their history."

The changer's mouth twists minutely, his hands ripple. For an instant, claws resolve from his fluxing flesh, but then the band on his leg glows bright gold. His shape resolves again, fingers blunt-edged and *safe*.

"Change can promote good," says Havander, his voice even.

"Yes, but not from humans," says Dacien, stopping. "And you know that better than most. You've seen first-hand the destruction they're capable of." He turns to me. "Did you see the old axe cuts in the Elder Tree on your way in?"

I remember them. I glance at Havander.

"They were made long ago by a desperate man," answers the changer. "The act itself was not malicious in nature."

"As you testified to the council," replies Dacien. "But they still punished you for letting him go. Was a year in the cells with your mind stripped worth it?"

The changer lifts his chin, all grace and unusual beauty. And whether or not he let one of their 'special' trees be damaged, my heart breaks for him.

Dacien sniffs. "Until Reeva meets with the council, you'll remain silent, Havander."

The changer's attention snaps to the wilder boy. Is that fear clouding them?

"There's no need to ensure it. I'll hold my tongue."

"It's best to be safe."

"NO!" cries out Havander.

But Dacien ignores him. He touches his bracelet and the band on Havander's leg illuminates in response. The changer grimaces as his chest brightens to brilliant blue. He doubles over and falls sideways. On the ground his form blurs and shivers; his robe contracts and melds to his body—an integral part of him.

Clothes from his own skin ...

His internal light flickers. His shape-change, when it happens, is jerky, not clean and quick like when he transformed from kingfisher to humanoid.

This is a forced morphing.

Dacien is *doing* this to him.

Horrified, I sink beside Havander. I don't dare touch him until his body has resolved. When it does, he is a blue-furred fox. Breaths rattle like river pebbles from his pointed muzzle. I rest my hand on his head. He settles.

"What the hell is wrong with you?" I snarl at Dacien. "Why did you do that to him?"

The wilder boy stalks forward—fluid, dangerous.

I surge to my feet.

"Don't assume to advise me on how best to deal with him," spits Dacien.

I lean in close. "I don't like bullies. You do that again in front of me, I'll knock you halfway into next week."

Dacien sneers, his perfect white teeth glittering in the light. "You can try."

I hate to say it, but I'm more like Dad than I care to admit.

My fist connects neatly with Dacien's jaw, returning a solid and satisfying *thunk*. I've never hit anyone before, and while it's not an exceptionally good punch, his head snaps sidewards and he stumbles. Palm to cheek, Dacien straightens. Fury and offence ripple across his face. Then his hand drops and he spits blood to one side.

"You're strong for a human," he says.

Not what I expected from him.

I rub my sore knuckles. "Always have been."

Dacien lifts his chin higher. He's chewing on words that for some reason remain unspoken.

"If you're finished," he says, finally, "keep moving."

He certainly has greater control over his emotions than I.

I linger for a moment, just to annoy him, then turn to the path.

The glistening citadel towers over the small, bustling township I saw earlier from the hill. Havander clings close to my heels as we walk the cobbled streets past dwellings built of stone and living tree roots, plaited and polished to a glossy shine. Everyday wilders go about their tasks, cooking, painting, gardening, and socialising—their inherent powers used to aid their industry. Each dwelling seems to have at least one changer in residence also, all in different forms—cats, horses, birds, humanoids—all with bands gleaming on their ankles.

One I notice, horse-shaped, hauls a cart piled high with straw bales. The wheels of the vehicle catch on the flagstones and the animal strains against the straps binding its chest. Its keeper yells and slaps a hand hard against the changer's flank. I frown at the treatment. The changer snorts and jostles forward, the cart once again moving. No one gives them a second look.

I decide I don't like these wilders all that much.

It's good to know your enemy though, so I keep my eyes open as we travel the streets. Cataloguing the types of wilders, at first glance, seems logical—at least from a physical standpoint. As elementals, they seem to fall into four distinct classes. Those with dark hair and blue eyes like Dacien are the water ones, I assume. Others are white-blond and green-eyed. They control earth I conclude as one places his palms to the ground only to have corn burgeon from the dirt moments later. Another one we pass with silver eyes and hair lounges in a chair on a verandah. Her whole form sways gently as if she's sitting in the middle of a summer breeze. Air wilder? Must be.

But the most interesting are those who sit about twenty metres above us on floating platforms nestled among the stalactites. I can just make out their details —the wild, red hair and sly yellow eyes. Their hands work metallic-red threads of fire that crackle and twist between their fingers. Embers surround them like a miasma of stars.

I'm still mad at Dacien, but curiosity gets the better of me. "What are they doing?" I ask.

"Fire weavers," he replies, tone clipped. "They keep the suns burning."

He offers nothing more and that's fine by me. Captivated, I watch them work until Havander bumps against my leg and whines. I look down. We have arrived at the citadel. It looms over us with its white granite walls sparkling and fine parapets covered in cascading red blooms of an unknown vine. Dacien takes the first of the ten wide steps that lead to huge double doors ornamented by the curl and sweep of living vines.

"This way," he instructs.

CHAPTER SEVEN

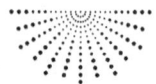

Greenery sprawls inside the building, flowers and fragrant leaves scenting the air with tones of vanilla and pepperberry. Polished woven tree roots, their still-living lengths carefully cultivated, form filigree type tables and chairs, artfully arranged throughout the high-ceilinged foyer.

Dacien halts at a pair of iron-banded doors at the far end. Their arched forms reach almost to the ceiling.

"Beyond is the audience gallery," he says, tone still cold. "Follow me and remain quiet. I'll present you and then you may plead your case." He points at Havander. "You wait outside."

I press my palm to the changer's head. He pushes against it reassuringly then trots away. The room seems colder without him. I wish he could have stayed.

The doors swing open at Dacien's touch and my eyesight adjusts to a change in the light. Beyond is a large circular hall, lit by a small fireball hovering high in the domed ceiling. Inside, the room is another kind of forest, one with brightness glancing off alabaster walls, polished wood, and shrouding greenery. A clean, clear stream chortles along the left side. It disappears into a natural crevice in the floor; the rush of a hidden waterfall marks its continued path below us.

But most impressive of all is the great old-growth eucalyptus dominating the centre of the room. It seems to almost whisper in a voice both ancient and forever—*I was the First Wilder and am the First Tree.*

I shake my head. The stress is getting to me.

A sandstone dais fronts the ragged-skirted gum. Four regal figures occupy it, seated resplendent on black granite thrones. Their matching golden robes and bracelets, like the one Dacien wears, all catch the light to full effect. To the far left of them, a fifth throne sits empty.

Of the assembled councillors, the tall, red-haired fire woman is the most distinctive. She lounges cat-like, her ease and confidence a striking contrast to that of her companions. She is as graceful as a cat, and all the way terrifying. A woman like that looks like she is used to getting what she wants.

The air wilder to her right, another woman, is older and bird-like in comparison. She perches on the edge of her seat; loose hair more iron grey than silver, sways gently in a breeze with seemingly no source. The fabric of her robe strikes glints in the depths of her shrewd mirror-like eyes. And they are shrewd for certain—two daggers to slice.

To her left is a man that could have been the Greek god, Apollo. Long white-blond hair kisses his shoulders and his eyes are the colour of clover. Arrogance bleeds from his heavy glare. His hands, bejewelled in amethyst rings, are broad and built like shovels. They hang loosely on the armrests. It's not hard to imagine them moulding earth or stone alike.

The last councillor has similar features to Dacien. He is shorter than the others and stocky, but no less handsome for it. He sits forward in his seat, open face intent on listening to an armour-clad, air woman standing on a lower platform.

"We saved the Elder Tree in the forest," says the soldier-woman, "but lost the other on the western flank of the river." She looks to the ground. "Most of my squad perished defending it."

The fire woman sits forward on her throne. "So the western access is now closed?"

"Yes, Councillor Hestia. We were overrun."

The earth wilder slams his palm on his thigh. "How could you let this happen? We're cut off from the coast and the Gordon River settlement!"

The soldier slumps. Her chain mail shirt, links shaped like leaves, clinks gently. "We retreated only to report the danger, Councillor Cephos. I shall return and continue to defend that ground should you wish it."

Cephos sneers and the one named Hestia raises her hand. "No, Lieutenant Aria. Return to the barracks and rest. Then, join the crew topside to secure more mounts. We need them to end this conflict swiftly."

Aria presses her hand to her chest and turns, fluid and graceful, to leave the platform. She pauses.

"Is there something else?" asks the old, air wilder woman.

"Yes, Councillor Zephyrine," says Aria, turning back. "We recovered a human. A male named Emmett. He's quarantined and with our healers now."

I hold my breath. Dad is already here?

Dacien glances at me and shakes his head. *Not the time to speak ...*

If my father is safe, I can wait.

Hestia frowns. "Was the man injured?"

"He will live," says Aria.

Something about the way she says it ... I'm missing something.

"You should have left it there, or killed it," says Cephos.

"No," says Hestia, looking thoughtful. "You've done well. Now go. We've much to consider."

The soldier bows and heads for the exit. As she passes us, the scent of old blood follows in her wake.

Councillor Hestia shifts in her seat, her mouth pinched tight. She glances up and her keen yellow gaze finds Dacien.

"Son," she says, sounding surprised. "Why are you here?"

Son? That's interesting.

"Mother," says Dacien. "I also bring news of a human caught in the skirmish topside tonight. Havander thought it prudent to rescue her. She comes seeking help to locate her father." He glances at the doors through which Aria just left. "But perhaps, we have already found him?"

Councillor Cephos's nose wrinkles. "By the Green God, another human? We are being overrun!"

I grit my teeth. "Please," I say. "Return my father to me, and we are more than happy to leave."

The earth wilder surges to his feet. Somewhere beneath us the ground rumbles. "You address me without invitation?"

"I meant no disrespect," I snap back.

Sparks of gold electricity crackle the length of the earth councillor's arm.

"And yet you are most disrespectful."

Dacien clears his throat. I ignore him.

"Forgive me, then," I say.

"Forgiving humans is like trying to forgive pigs for their love of mud."

I lose my patience. "Your insults mean nothing to me."

Cephos clenches his hand into a fist and the floor beneath me groans and cracks. Dacien dances backwards. The crack widens.

"I'll not be spoken to like that by a top dweller," growls the councillor.

"Cephos! NO!" cries Hestia.

But the earth wilder pays no heed. His wrist twists and the floor beneath me crumbles away. An abrupt sense of weightlessness has me cry out, and I instinctively throw up both hands. Cutting pain pierces my left wrist and a sudden silver light blinds me. I land on something hard with a small thump.

A sudden gasp—maybe it's Zephyrine—urgent mutters follow.

My vision clears and I find myself suspended over a deep crevasse cut into the floor. My boots balance on what seems to be a horizontal, translucent sheet of sparkling light, thin as air.

I should have fallen.

How the hell didn't I?

The councillors seem to be wondering the same thing. They all stare at me, shocked. Cephos, wide-eyed, stumbles backwards and drops into his seat. The hole in the floor closes.

I blink and the light holding me aloft fades. I drop back to solid ground.

"Guards," screeches Zephyrine, "seize her!"

CHAPTER EIGHT

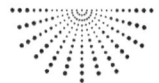

I'm given no chance to speak, no chance to ask questions. Instead, I am dragged through a side door by two burly earth wilders and marched down a dim corridor lined with doors.

"Where are you taking me?" I snarl, struggling against my captors' firm grip. "What did I do?"

They don't answer, their fair faces as impervious as stone.

The last door is my destination. Pulled open by the left hand guard, I am shoved through. I swivel, angry, pulling a loose strand of hair from my mouth.

The guards retreat without a word, the door lock clicking closed behind them.

I scream, frustrated. The sound bounces impotent off the stone walls.

What am I going to do now?

I survey the room, looking for something to try and break the door. A single couch with a woven root frame hugs one wall. A small desk sits opposite, a carved timber stool beside it. A single lamp hangs from the vaulted ceiling, too far to reach. This room looks like a halfway space—a waiting area.

I guess that means I'm expected to wait.

The couch is soft as I lean back into it. My thoughts race as I flick my fingernails against each other. I can't explain what happened to me back in the council hall. I rub my still-aching wrist, skipping along the raised edge left by Havander's healing. The pain there resonates deep, like ice pressed against the bone.

I breathe out and focus on the silence of the room. I'm at the mercy of these people but that doesn't mean I'm powerless.

Footsteps sound outside in the corridor, accompanied by the quiet jangle of armour. The guards are approaching again.

"Open up," says a deep voice.

The door cracks and I glimpse a flash of gold behind it. The water wilder councillor pushes into the room. In such a small space, he seems larger than he did sitting on the dais outside. His sapphire-coloured eyes rake the room then fall on me.

"Dacien tells us your name is Reeva," he says.

"That's right."

He turns to the guard that led him here. "You may leave us."

The wilder nods and the door closes again. The councillor waits until the sound of retreating footsteps has faded away.

"I am Councillor Neru." His cheek catches the fickle

light as he lifts his chin. "The only one on the council who doesn't want to kill you right now."

I wither inside, my stomach turning to jelly.

"Why do they want me dead? I've done nothing wrong."

Neru's brow furrows. "I'm all for breaking rules, but you were too cavalier. You should never have revealed what you are."

"What I am? I'm just a girl."

"We both know you are far more than that."

Tears bite. "I don't know what you are talking about!"

Neru frowns. He crosses his arms. "You really don't know?"

"Know WHAT?" I cry, frustrated.

"Reeva," he says in a way that suggests he doesn't believe me. "You're a hybrid. Why one of my kind would create you, I don't know, but here, in The Styx, you are considered an abomination. Surely you knew this? That's why they want you dead."

"Dead?"

"Yes."

The walls loom close. Has the temperature dropped? Every part of me screams to run, but where?

"What the hell is a hybrid?" I ask.

Neru's head tilts as he considers me. "You're half human, half a water wilder."

"I'm nothing that special. Please just let me go."

"I can't." Long moments pass. "Why would you ever choose to come here?"

"I didn't. I was brought here."

Neru's gaze drops.

"What's going to happen to me?"

"Well, Reeva, that depends on you. I've a proposition for you to consider. It's the one chance you have to save yourself."

Why do I get the feeling that, once again, the course of my life will be charted by the needs of others?

"Why are you helping me?"

Neru clasps his hands together. "There is change in the wind. I think maybe you can help us navigate that."

"And that's enough?"

"I've nothing to lose exploring the idea."

"And I get to live a little longer."

"Exactly."

"Okay," I say. "I'm listening."

Neru perches himself on the stool by the desk. His gown pools like molten metal around his feet.

"I've convinced my colleagues of your value. In return for your service, they have agreed to grant you freedom, and in time, return your father to you. He is the human they found in the forest, is he not?"

"Yes."

"Good. I'm glad he is safe." Neru nods as if satisfied. "Now, to understand what we will ask of you, you first need to grasp the nature of our existence."

"Okay."

Neru raises his hand to encompass the room and I get the sense, what is beyond it also. "This city and the caverns beneath The Styx Valley were created by the first wilder thousands of years ago. These are our ancestral lands and we are the custodians of the natural elements. With our powers, we are ordained to protect the planet."

The burbling cadence of his voice holds an intoxicating storyteller's quality.

"The Elder Trees are the doorways to our world." He twists his wrist and light spills from his palm. It flows like mercury, forming silvery shapes that hover mid-air—illustrations to his tale. First, a magnificent *Eucalyptus regenes* solidifies.

"The changers you saw topside want these entrances destroyed," he says. "These creatures can shapeshift to look human and they use this power to work change in the world above to free it of our influence. If they succeed, they will see us buried alive in our cities, helpless to protect the forests."

The fluid image changes again. This time the great tree shudders. Moving effigies of changers rise at the base, their forms morphing between the now familiar bald-headed creatures and that of humans. Axes are clasped in their hands. They swing at the tree. The forest king falls to the ground and shatters into droplets. The images fade away.

"Understand that changers blend in. They encourage humans to grow, to build and develop in ways that would see everything we work to uphold, destroyed." Neru taps his bracelet. "This is why we keep the changers safely contained here below ground."

"What has all this got to do with me?" I whisper,

unsettled by the thought of any life lived, bound by chains.

Neru's eyes glitter. "The changers who attacked you and your father are a sizeable group who rebelled against us. They somehow removed their anklets and fled the cavern system. As you heard tonight, they have already cut one of our two Elder Trees down. An incalculable loss to us. And now, the council has received demands that the rest of the changers be released or the last tree remaining will fall also. Should we comply with their demands, they'll eventually lead humanity to destroy the planet. We deny them, and they take our last entrance."

"And the world above will die without you?"

"Yes."

"Why do you think I can make a difference?"

Neru shrugs. "We wilders are limited. We are unable to spend extended amounts of time topside. If we do, our powers fade and we become human. As a hybrid, you have no such limitation. You are a child of both worlds. I believe you could be invaluable in helping to defuse the situation before it turns into outright war."

Havander may be the only civilised example I have, but he has only ever shown me kindness. "Are the changers really that bad?" I ask. "Why can't you negotiate with them? Surely granting them freedom is better than waging war?"

"Your compassion is admirable, Reeva, but we can't entertain negotiations." The lines of his face deepen.

"We'll not free the changers. We know their nature better than you. The risk is too great."

"And I can't be party to slavery or murder," I say. "I just can't do it."

Neru lifts his chin. "Then consider your own position. You are in our domain. You are a hybrid. Our laws call for you to be executed."

It's a thinly veiled threat. I swallow.

"Say I help. What happens when everything resolves?"

"Show your loyalty and the council will be convinced that your human half is not something to be feared. Show us that we *can* work with humanity, not against it. And with your access to the upper world, you could perhaps become our representative—the face of a new collaboration."

"You almost sound like Havander."

"I am no changer, but born of water I am mutable. That is the difference. Flexing rules is different to breaking them."

"I don't really have a choice here, do I?"

"Of course you do."

"The other option?"

"Zephyrine is calling for your death at sunrise."

I press my lips thin. This is extortion.

"All right. I'll do it, but I want to see my father first."

Neru releases a breath, one he seems to have been holding. "I understand, but I can't allow it just yet. He is gravely injured and needs time to heal. He is being treated with all respect and care. Once stable, I'll take you myself to visit him."

"How long?"

"I'm uncertain," says Neru. "But in the meantime, Hestia has, on your acceptance of this proposal, offered quarters to you in her home."

The scary fire-lady. Great.

"Thanks."

"And we will begin work on your magic," says Neru. "Your instinctive use of it will need to be honed."

"Am I really magic?"

Neru smiles, all traces of his previous threat gone. "You proved it today in the hall."

My magic. Such a strange concept. But when I consider it, I know somewhere deep inside, that it's true. The seed of something unusual has always lingered just beneath my skin—my uncommon strength, my uncanny draw to the forest—just symptoms of something much larger than I ever understood.

"But I don't know how to make it work," I say, suddenly concerned. "That light thing I did, it's not something that's ever happened before.

"Don't fear. We will help you refine your gift."

"You can do that?"

"Yes, but you've survived an ordeal and first need rest. Come and I'll take you to your lodgings."

He's right. I'm exhausted. I nod and Neru quietly leads me from the room, out through the now empty council chamber and into the town.

I've never looked more forward to rest than I do right now.

CHAPTER NINE

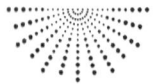

Cocooned in sleep, I dream of Galen Mayer. He is out of uniform, instead dressed like a wilder. I don't know why he's on my mind. Maybe our interaction yesterday brings back old feelings, or maybe, considering my situation, I'm wishing for law enforcement intervention. Either way, the dream is strange. We're standing opposite each other, a large dark hole bored into the earth between us. Galen holds a stone in his hand.

"What is it?" I ask.

Galen's chip drops, his sorrow palpable. "Something I loved and lost."

It hurts to see him so forlorn. I reach for him across the pit.

"Don't worry," I reply. "You can love me instead."

His eyes meet mine and a smile curls his lips.

I wake with a jolt, heart hammering, and cheeks burning. I press a hand to my chest. Even asking "dream" Galen to love me is enough to mortify. He'd never be interested in someone like me—a half-human weirdo. With both hands, I brush back my hair and take a deep breath. I remind myself that I'm in Hestia's house. Galen is far away.

A wash of light sweeps past the bedroom window, coming from a small sun outside, drifting close. It spills warmth and illumination across the woollen blankets covering the bed. I push away the lingering image of Galen, stretch my arms and crack my neck.

My opinion of the room has changed since last night when Neru and Dacien brought me here. It had seemed cold with its washed-out décor—the white walls, silvery timber bedframes and raw woollen blankets, all too white and too perfect. I was afraid to touch anything. The little sun, with its red-yellow light, has gone a long way to make it seem more welcoming.

My thoughts turn to Dad. I wonder how he is this morning and hope he's okay. Probably giving the healers hell to be honest. I don't envy them one little bit. I throw back the blanket and swing my legs out. The floor is cold against my feet. I head to the small washbasin and mirror set into a wall alcove by the window. My reflection stares back at me. Dark circles mark the skin beneath my grey eyes. My black hair hangs mussed around my high cheekbones.

So I'm half wilder. I don't see it. I lean in closer but find only the features I've always had. I look like my father I'm told and I guess I do have the same shaped chin as him. I can only guess at what parts look like my long-lost mother.

My wilder mother.

I sure as hell have a lot of questions for Dad when I see him next.

I splash water across my face. The cool slap jolts me to alertness. With the brush that sits to one side, I worry the tangles free from my hair and tie it into a ponytail.

I eye off my dress where it hangs over a chair. Even as comfortable as it is, I really hate dresses. A wardrobe in the corner looks promising though. Hopeful, I stalk across and open it. Within hang three pairs of black leggings and tight-fitted dark blue shirts, similar to what Dacien wears. Grateful, I choose a set and shrug myself in.

I'm pulling on my boots when I hear a quiet knock.

"It's just me," says Dacien.

"Come in."

The door creaks open and the boy enters, wearing a simple black jerkin and leggings. The silver bracelet flashes on his wrist. The shadow of a bruise marks his cheek where I struck him, but he still manages to look like he just stepped out of a salon.

"I've been instructed to assess your abilities," he states, aloof.

Great.

Why couldn't it have been Neru? At least he doesn't hate me.

"I'm about as excited at the prospect, as you are," I reply.

"I doubt it," he says, lifting his chin sharply. "I should be out helping my people prepare for what's coming, but instead Neru has insisted and my mother, albeit with hesitation, has agreed. As such, we have no choice but to work together."

"Well, let's get this over with then. The faster we work, the quicker we'll be out of each other's lives."

"Agreed." He nods and holds out a thick biscuit. "Breakfast," he says. "Small but it will sustain you."

"What is it?"

"A ration brick. Seeds and dried fruit. We use them when away from the valley."

I take it and nibble at the edge. It's tasty. I glance back at him. "Have you heard anything else about my dad?"

"No," says Dacien, shifting on his feet. "But news will come when there is a change."

I sigh, swallowing my disappointment. "All right then," I say. "I guess I'm ready to go when you are."

Hestia's home is designed much like a Roman villa. Long, wide corridors are lined on one side with glass doors, all leading to an internal, tiled courtyard. Columns of woven roots and lush greenery circle the open space. Birdsong plays from amongst the plants. I glimpse the bright blue plumage of a Superb Fairy Wren.

Havander, in his humanoid form, waits for us near a white stone well at the centre of the yard. He looks calm this morning, the forced changing yesterday seeming not to have affected his health. His hands are neatly clasped together at his front.

"Good morning, Reeva," he greets, bowing his head. His grey robes flutter with the movement, the anklet on his leg sparkles.

"Morning, Havander."

Dacien ignores the changer. He turns. "Now, hybrid," he says without preamble. "As a half-blood, we can't be sure how powerful you actually are. We will first work on basic skills—shield formation and weapon making. They're relatively easy to master and with them, at the very least, you'll be able to both protect yourself *and* kill rebel changers."

I glance at Havander, uncomfortable. He remains impassive.

Dacien extends his arm, his hand curled into a fist. "Stand like this. Search for the natural currents that ride just below your skin. Reach for them."

I try to do as he asks. I stand there but sense nothing other than the slow *bu-bump, bu-bump* of my own heartbeat.

"Dig deeper, hybrid."

That word again. *Hybrid*. Like I'm only worth half of something.

"Stop calling me that," I say.

"What? Hybrid? But that's what you are."

"Yeah? Well you're arrogant and rude but I don't call you an arsehole," I reply.

Dacien glowers.

"Reeva, then," he says. "Try again. The power feels like bees under your skin."

I focus and this time find it, a thrumming but only in my left arm. The buzz quickens. Faster. Faster. Deep in the well, the water gurgles. Did I do that? A sharp pain lances through my scar.

"Ouch! It hurts," I say.

"It shouldn't," says Dacien.

"Well, it does."

The wilder boy frowns. "Probably something to do with your human blood."

Arsehole.

He roughly grasps my wrist and turns it over.

"I can only feel the sensation in the one arm," I say.

Dacien purses his mouth. His finger runs across my scar and then he looks at Havander. "You healed this wound for her?"

The changer nods.

"Your injury," says the boy. "Residue from Havander's power has bonded with your hybrid blood along the seam. Look, here. I've not seen anything like it before."

I lean over. Barely visible is a network of blue threads interwoven through the raised flesh.

"It's effectively formed a gateway in the human barrier through which your power can exit," he continues. "That's probably why you've never been able to use it before now." He shrugs. "As it stands, you'll only be able to wield magic from this one hand unless you wish to cut the other one open and have it healed also?"

I shake my head. "I'm not the kind of girl that thinks scars are cool."

Dacien lets go of my arm. "Well, you'll be weaker for it. But one arm is better than none. Let's try again."

～

Mid-afternoon, and I'm completely over magic. I've tried a thousand different ways to make the power manifest again but other than creating a few sparks in my palm I've achieved nothing. It's beyond frustrating.

Havander sits on the edge of the well looking bored and Dacien, exasperated, pinches the bridge of his nose. He sighs and his hand drops.

"Okay, Reeva," he says, trying, I think, to act calmer than he is. He clasps my wrist. His fingers ignite and the cold flame of his power caresses my forearm. "Try and focus on what my power feels like," he continues. "See how it doesn't burn? It's cool. Close your eyes and just sit with it."

I do as he asks. His magic against my skin is a pleasant sensation, and very different from the pain I feel anytime I try to conjure it for myself.

"Expand your senses," says Dacien. "Reach for the moisture in the well."

The water whispers to me from the darkness below the rim. Its presence ripples gently against my awareness. I take stock of it and note the dissolved minerals in its matrix and the gentle sway of the algae it houses.

"Good," says Dacien. "Now try and extend your power through your arm. Gather the liquid. Form a sphere above the well with it."

I reach with my mind. Fire cuts through my scar.

It's hotter than ever. The more I try to wrestle with the magic, the more it hurts. I clench my hand and open my eyes.

"I can't do it," I sob.

"You CAN!" yells Dacien. "You already have!" He snatches his hand away. "You aren't trying hard enough."

"Dacien," says Havander calmly. "Perhaps a small break?"

The wilder boy waves a hand. "Good idea. I need a moment. You wait here with her."

"Of course," says Havander.

Dacien taps his bracelet and Havander's anklet illuminates, its controlling power activated. Dacien then spins on his heel and stalks away. His disappointment in the morning's work is evident in the slump of his shoulders. I can't say I blame him. I'm frustrated with the lack of progress too.

Havander watches Dacien enter the house. He rubs his anklet like it hurts him, and then straightens.

"Without control of your magic," he says, "you'll be in danger topside. I can perhaps teach you something more tangible to help with that."

"What were you thinking?" I ask, rubbing my aching arm.

Havander settles into a combatant's stance, hands straight, elbows pointed out slightly.

"You look like a ninja," I say.

"What's a ninja?"

"A type of kick-arse human fighter."

Havander smirks and for an instant I'm reminded

of Galen back in high school—the way he always made me feel like I wasn't an outsider. Havander has the same quality.

"Not human, so not a ninja. Sorry!" he says. "But I *can* show you how to physically defend yourself."

I copy the changer's stance. "I stand like this?"

"Exactly like that," he says.

I grin, eager for the change of pace. "Let's do this."

CHAPTER TEN

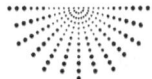

The afternoon with Havander has left me bruised and battered, but in a good way. I'm not sure where he learnt to fight, but he's skilful. He's taught me how to swing both a high and low kick and how to throw someone over my shoulder. Only a few moves but they give me confidence. I'll keep practising.

After a hot bath, I'm clean and ready for dinner. I've chosen to wear the dress that Dacien made me, mainly because Hestia's very formal invitation, delivered by her personal changer maid, made choosing anything else feel inappropriate. I smooth the wrinkles from the skirt one last time and ease out of my room. To the right, down the corridor, is the dining room Havander pointed out earlier today. As I pass the glass doors leading to the courtyard, I notice the fire-suns in the caverns have dimmed, leaving an ethereal gloom outside that resembles night.

Hestia and Dacien are already eating when I arrive. The table is laden with plates of cheeses, fruit, breads and two carafes, one filled with water, the other with blood-red wine. The two wilders sit at opposite ends to each other, a cold arrangement that suggests a formal relationship between the mother and son. It's weird. Dad and I don't use the dining room at home. Instead we choose the verandah where we sit on patchwork couches and eat from plates balanced on our laps.

"Reeva," greets Hestia. "Come in."

This is the first time I've seen the fire councillor since the council chamber. Up close, her ivory skin is flawless and her uncanny, yellow eyes, when they catch mine, scorch. I swallow to compose myself. She is beautiful, like all wilders are, but, unlike the others, she holds a predatory edge to her lines, the same way as a tiger snake does.

Hestia is dangerous.

She taps the arm of the chair next to her.

"Sit," she says, her voice low and smoky. "I'm pleased you have joined us."

"Thanks for the invite," I say, holding my tone firm. I cross the room, my nerves on edge and senses held alert. I slide back the chair and sit. This close to the fire councillor, the air temperature has risen by at least two degrees.

"Liander," calls Hestia over her shoulder.

From the shadows against the rear wall, a changer approaches, carrying a covered platter. I recognise her as the one who delivered Hestia's invitation to me earlier. She sets the plate down gently in front of me, and then hands me the knife and fork from the table as if I can't pick them up myself.

"Thank you, Liander," I say, uncomfortable with being waited on and determined to acknowledge her as something more than a slave.

A small smile curls Liander's lips. She nods her thanks and then retreats.

I lift the lid and my mouth waters at the rising scent of cooked vegetables. Piled high on the plate are roast potatoes, steamed beans, snow peas, and a pile of boiled green leaves that looks suspiciously like spinach. I hate spinach. I poke at it with the fork.

"Dandelion greens," says Hestia, her tone almost motherly. "Very healthy for you."

I don't care how healthy they are. They look awful, but I don't want to be rude.

"Thank you." I take a forkful. They're bitter.

Dacien smirks, obviously enjoying my discomfort.

After a delicate bite of beans, Hestia clears her throat.

"It's not often we entertain the company of a hybrid."

"Never, in fact," mutters Dacien.

Hestia glares at him. "And that is exactly why we are thrilled you are here."

What does she expect me to say to that? *Thanks for not killing me ...*

"I'm thankful for your hospitality," I manage to say.

Hestia smiles—all cupid bow lips. "We would love to learn more about you."

I'm not really in the mood to divulge anything to her, but remind myself to be polite. "What would you like to know?"

Hestia leans back from her plate. "Anything to know you better," says Hestia. "Tell us about yourself and what it's like to live as a human. Do you live close by? How did you grow up? Do you have other family?"

I take a bite of potato to wash away the taste of the greens. A sip of water from a glass next to me also helps.

"I live with my dad on our farm, Tarina. It's not too far away. No other family. We breed Shetland ponies."

"I see," says Hestia. "Is there no human step-mother wondering where you are?"

"No, it's only Dad and myself."

But that doesn't mean we are alone, lady.

"The police will know we are missing though," I continue. "We were meant to meet them on the night I arrived here. They'll be out looking for us."

Hestia sips her glass of wine. Her bracelet sparks, the edges catching the light from the candles arrayed in the centre of the table. "The Maydena police force?"

"You know them?" I ask, surprised.

"I've heard of them," she says, an edge to her voice. She offers no explanation and I get the sense I shouldn't ask for one.

I take another bite. For a plate of simple vegetables, they are full of flavour—spicy pepper and garlic.

"What was your life like growing up?" asks Hestia, suddenly. "It can't have been easy fitting in, being what you are."

"My lack of fitting in had nothing to do with being a hybrid," I say around another mouthful of beans.

"What do you mean?"

Why all these deep and meaningful personal questions? I get the sense Hestia's not the type to be polite for polite's sake. I straighten and place my fork down. "It's really not that exciting. Are you sure you're interested?"

"Of course," says Hestia, leaning forward. "Do forgive me if I'm making you uncomfortable. It's just that I find humans fascinating. They're full of complexity."

Her eyes are brighter—she's lying. What's her game? I swallow.

"Well, there isn't much to know," I say. "I'm an only child. I grew up with a father who was accused, but never convicted, of murdering my mother. Losing her broke him. Life, as you can imagine, was lonely."

Silence holds the room like a blanket. Hestia's wilder mask sits intact but something … something … flutters at the edges of her mouth.

"I am sorry to hear that," she says, finally. "Your father was, no doubt, lucky to have you, and you, him."

"Something like that," I say.

Dacien clears his throat.

Hestia blinks as if woken from a reverie. She straightens. "Enough said. Tell me how are things progressing with your powers?" she asks. "Any break-throughs?"

I glance at Dacien.

"No, Mother," he says. "Reeva struggles. There's pain in her wrist when she tries to manifest her magic."

"I see," says Hestia. "Show me."

I hold out my arm. My scar shines white-blue in the candlelight.

Hestia rises from her seat and gently grasps my arm. Her skin is uncomfortably hot against mine.

"This mix of changer and hybrid magic is unusual," she says. "But I can see how the bridge is formed."

She releases my arm. "Perhaps I can help you find your way."

With a flick of her wrist, the fire from the candles on the table flies to her hand. The flames gather in her palm.

"Try and focus on the sound of your power. For myself, it's the quiet rush of rising heat." Her yellow gaze drops to her hand. She breathes out and her power ignites, spinning like a tiny tornado in her grasp. The movement condenses the flames into a tight, bright ember. She then presses her hand closed and opens it. A translucent bubble forms down the length of her right arm, glittering gold, threaded through with sparks of fire.

"A shield," she says, "The easiest of creations. It can protect, but can also be a tool." She closes her hand again and the shield retracts to circle her fist. She flicks her hand and sends it sailing through the air. The bubble hovers over my glass for a moment and splashes into it. The water inside spills over the rim and onto the table.

Hestia tilts her head and stretches her fingers. The shield in the glass bulges. The vessel trembles under the force, and then shatters. Glass slivers land by my plate.

"See?" says Hestia. "You just need to use your imagination."

Imagination? When I use my power, it's ibuprofen I need. I rub my wrist.

"I've tried everything, Mother," says Dacien. "She can't get past the pain."

Hestia's shield fades and she returns to her seat. "A shame. But persist. I'm sure you'll both get there."

I frown, watching as Dacien flicks his hand. The fluid Hestia left on the table dissipates into mist.

"I'll keep trying," I say.

A quiet knock taps at the dining room door.

"Anyone home?" asks a familiar voice.

Neru enters, followed by Havander. The water councillor is dressed in dark blue breeches and doublet. The colour matches his eyes.

"Neru," greets Hestia, her voice warm. "Welcome. Do join us."

Neru raises his hand. "Please, don't stop on my account. I have already eaten this evening."

He takes the chair next to me. "I've just come to check in on Reeva."

"As you can see," says Hestia. "She is well."

"And the training?"

"Don't ask," says Dacien.

I scowl at him.

"It's only the first day," says Neru. "And you've never trained a hybrid before, Dacien. There are bound to be some complexities to it. Don't lose faith yet."

Dacien doesn't look convinced.

"Are there any updates on my dad?" I ask, really

wanting to move past conversations about my failure. "Can I see him yet?"

"A straight-to-the-point kind of girl," says Neru, chuckling. "I like that."

"Well?"

"Unfortunately, not yet," Neru pops a grape into his mouth, chews and swallows. "Your father's recovery is complicated. He's taken ill with an infection. The healers are confident he'll recover, but stress that he needs rest. A little longer and then you can see him."

Disappointment sours my stomach. Neru places a hand on my shoulder and squeezes.

"I understand your frustration, but don't worry yourself. He is receiving the best of care." He reaches over and grabs the carafe of wine. Filling an empty glass, he then takes a sip.

Neru leans back into his seat. "You're best to focus on your work. Solstice approaches. Let's get these escaped changers back into the fold and then everything else will be resolved."

I want to believe him. I do.

But something about all this just doesn't sit right.

Why can't I see Dad?

CHAPTER ELEVEN

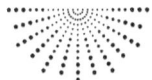

Only Day Two underground and it already feels like I've been here forever. I roll my shoulders and take a deep breath. We are back in the courtyard again and Dacien seems refreshed—not nearly as moody as yesterday.

I rub my hands down the front of my shirt. "I'm ready."

Dacien nods. "Like yesterday, focus," he says. "Imagine a bubble in your palm. This is the base building block of your shield. It doesn't matter how large or small it is. We'll practice adjusting the size."

Right. A shield.

Just call me Lagertha, Viking shield-maiden.

I concentrate on my scar. The slide of magic beneath my skin is easy to find and the water in the well feels close also. I visualise the pale fire Dacien wields and how it would look spilling from my seamed flesh and across my palm.

Familiar pain bites. I skate over it, telling myself it's

only a distraction. An ephemeral resonance draws my attention and as Hestia suggested, I imagine sounds of water.

The splash of waves.

Raindrops against a windscreen.

The drip of Dad's blood against the dash of the car.

My concentration falters.

I blink.

The courtyard has transformed. I'm standing in the heart of a sphere, water droplets floating suspended around me, their perfect, tiny beads illuminated like diamonds. My entire left hand is encased in a ball of cold silver-white flames.

I grin like a crazy girl—success feels like madness—but the lines of Dacien's face stay pinched.

"Are you seeing this?" I ask. "I did it!"

"Yes," replies Dacien with a sigh. "I see your shield, as big as the garden."

"You don't seem impressed."

"Your power is unstable."

"Can't you just be excited I got this far?"

The wilder waves a hand at the plants. It's then I realise their leaves have all shrivelled.

"I'll be excited," he says, "when you don't wither away half a forest in the bid to gather moisture."

I let the magic fade and the droplets dissipate.

"I'm sorry," I mutter. "I didn't mean to do that."

Dacien shakes his head. In his palm, threads of power ignite. They gently extend, gathering the moisture and turning it into mist. The white cloud expands and coils across the ground and towards the garden. At its touch, the plants replenish, leaves plumping to become whole again. My mistake is wiped clean.

"Our skill is not only the drawing of moisture to us," says Dacien. "It's about giving back also. A balance must always be maintained."

I remember the dress he made me. "What about the clothes then? How did you give to make them?"

"The foundation material was drawn from the well," says Dacien, "a vessel specifically created to hold water not yet in use—so nothing was stolen. Technically, we can take moisture from the air, from the earth, plants and even living bodies if we must, but such actions are a deprivation to the source. It is always better to use rain, river water or a well's bounty to manipulate."

It makes sense. Don't use moisture that something else is using first. I look at my hand.

"The power," I say. "How do you inherit control over a specific element?"

"What do you mean?" replies Dacien.

"Well …" I bite my lip. "You're a water wilder. Were you born with these powers or were they selected somehow for you?"

"Why would you ask that?"

I shrug. "I'd like to understand how I came to be like I am."

Dacien's gaze softens. "We're born with it," he says, finally. "The genetics of the mother determines the ability. The fathers give nothing in this regard. For example, fire mothers always give birth to water children. Earth breeds fire, water breeds air and air breeds earth."

"So because Hestia controls fire, you control water?"

"Correct."

"So that means my mum would have been like her too?"

"Of course."

That small piece of information settles around me. The first concrete detail I've ever gleaned about my mother. Other questions crowd in. How did my father meet her? What really happened to her? Is this how Dad knew about the changers?

"How did you not already know this?" asks Dacien.

"My father never talked about her, and I was too scared to ask him."

The hard lines framing Dacien's mouth disappear. "I didn't realise," he says. "I thought you were aware of your heritage and were lying—being cautious to protect yourself."

I shake my head. "I'm no liar, but I am cautious. I'm out of my depth here and worried about my dad."

Havander, standing at his place by the well, straightens. "Your father will be all right, Reeva," he says. "Neru has given his word."

Dacien nods. "What's been promised will be honoured."

"I hope so," I say.

"You care a lot about your father, don't you?" asks Dacien.

"Don't you care about your family?"

"I do," says Dacien. He pauses. "But while we have parents and love them, the natural world is our priority. It comes before all else. Besides, my father died some time ago."

"I'm sorry to hear that."

"Don't be. It doesn't affect me."

These wilders have a coolness to them that rattles me. How could anyone be so driven by a singular, material purpose that it would transcend love and compassion?

A pretty sad way to live in my opinion.

"Tell me," I ask. "Do you think my mother returned here all those years ago? Could she still be here?"

Dacien shrugs. "I don't know. She would've carefully hidden her secret. Wilders found concealing such children are severely punished."

"Why would she have me then?"

"We can only speculate," says Dacien. "Maybe she didn't have the heart to turn you in, or perhaps she saw a use for you as Neru does. Maybe she thought you could save the world."

"I'm no superhero."

"But you *are* strong." He presses a finger to his still-bruised cheek and smirks.

I smirk back.

Dacien glances down, as if considering his next words carefully.

"You really should be grateful for the opportunity you've been given here."

"Opportunity?"

He lifts his chin. "The escaped changers are a minor threat that will soon be resolved," he says. "But the greater battle for the protection of this planet is ongoing. We wilders are only so many, and the damage done already great. We need help."

He isn't wrong about the world above. I flex my left hand, wondering if I will ever be able to control my magic enough to help.

Dacien must read my mind. His touch is cool as he gently grasps my fingers and folds them over into a fist.

"You can make a shield now," he says. "That is a good start. I'll show you how to manipulate the size of it. Then we'll work on weapons."

I'm not sure what has inspired his sudden kindness, or this sudden faith in me.

"You really think I can master this?"

He smiles. "Yes, and when you do, you'll help both your father and the wilder people."

I take a deep breath and close my eyes.

But I am keenly aware of Havander still standing silent by the well.

If I do succeed, what happens to his people?

Do they continue to live and die in chains?

CHAPTER TWELVE

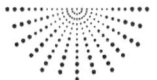

Day three and 'stir-crazy' has started to set in. I've not been allowed to leave the house. *For my own protection,* I'm told. *A hybrid walking alone through the streets would be attacked, or worse.*

It's the afternoon and Dacien has called it for today. He's been surprisingly patient since my breakthrough and I'm thankful for his shift in attitude. But the hours spent manipulating water shields and failing to craft an actual weapon has left me exhausted.

I sink onto my bed, ignoring the ache centred around the scar on my arm.

"Reeva?"

Havander slides into my room. He carries a basket filled with fruit and fresh baked goods. My stomach gurgles with hunger.

"Hestia and Dacien are both busy this evening," says Havander. "Dinner will be in your room tonight."

I don't mind the break. It means I don't have to

dress up and hear more excuses as to why I can't see Dad.

"That bread smells delicious," I say.

"It's still warm." The changer places the basket next to my bed.

I grab an apple first, relishing the crunch of it between my teeth.

"I've no set tasks this evening," says Havander, his hands crossed before him.

I note his anklet is glowing. No powers again. Dacien must have given him permission to be here.

"If you like," says the changer, "I can take you out for a walk after you eat."

I stop, mid-chew. "Really?" I say around my mouthful. "I thought it wasn't safe for me to leave the house."

"You'll have nothing to fear if I'm with you," he says.

Escaping my confines, even just for a little while, is too tempting to refuse. "Where would we go?"

Havander grins. "I've somewhere special in mind."

I need a nice surprise. I finish the apple and grab a piece of bread to go.

"I'm all yours," I say.

Outside the streets are busy and the air is filled with the scent of roasting vegetables and the sizzle of fried flatbreads. Meat isn't on the menu anywhere in this place. With only carbs and greens as my steady diet, I salivate at the thought of a medium-rare steak.

The fire wilders are winding down their industry

for the day. The suns they maintain now hang low in the valley, dull and red. Soon the night-like gloom will descend again.

Havander leads me past the more affluent houses and heads for the river. In the distance the old ruins I first noticed on arrival rise from the opposite bank, broken teeth of grey stone above the tannin brown water. The air feels colder here too.

We turn at the end of town, and towards a large building fashioned from roots. No effort has been wasted here to polish them smooth. A familiar smell lingers over the place—a mix of horse manure and hay.

"Where are we?" I ask.

Havander smiles but says nothing. He pushes open a small side entrance. Warm lamplight and the quiet nickers of horses filter through. I step inside to find a generous stable complete with work areas past the stalls. I survey the rows of neatly corralled animals. There are at least a hundred mounts here and the closest is Rosco, one of the Anderson's prize stallions.

I grin and grasp Havander's wrist in tight fingers. "The stolen horses?"

The changer's eyes dance with mischief. "We shouldn't be here, but your Echo has been missing you."

I press my lips together, suddenly suspicious. "Are you trying to butter me up for something?"

"Butter you up?"

"Do something nice for me," I explain, "so you can ask for something in return?"

"On my word," says Havander, "I'll not ask you for anything related to butter."

Funny. I chuckle. "Well in that case, where is she?"

"Ten stalls down."

Echo's welcome is a high-pitched nicker. She reaches over the rail to snuff eagerly at my pockets for the apple I usually bring her, but don't have this time. I run my hand down her smooth grey nose. Her presence is a desperate reminder of home—her familiarity almost breaking me. I press my forehead to her nose, biting back tears.

"I'm sorry, girl. We can't leave yet."

Echo snorts, her humid breath carrying scents of lucerne and grain. I tangle my fingers into her mane and pretend for a moment that we never left Tarina, and this is all just a bad dream.

"Are you all right?" asks Havander quietly. "I thought you'd be happy to see her."

I lift my head. "I am," I say. "It's just I'm reminded of Dad and home."

Havander's gaze drops away. "I'm sorry. If not for me, you'd be home right now."

"Without you I wouldn't know that Dad was here safe, and that would be worse."

The changer stands quiet for a moment. When he speaks, his voice is barely a whisper.

"You don't owe them anything, you know."

"Who? The wilders? What choice do I have?"

Havander shrugs. "You've seen the circumstances of my own people. You could help us instead."

I sigh. As much as I abhor his situation, I'm in no position to go against his captors.

"How, Havander? They have Dad and have threatened to kill me if I don't tow the line."

The creases around his mouth deepen. "You're a brave and clever girl, Reeva. If you chose to, you could somehow make a difference for us, I just know it. But right now, they're using you. You're no less a slave than I am."

Deep in my gut, I know he's right.

"You've listened to what they've had to say. Hear our side of the story too," says Havander, "and if afterwards you want to maintain your course of current action, I'll respect that."

Echo turns to her feed bucket.

"Please?"

I consider the changer's request. It can't hurt to understand what lies on both sides of the fence.

"Okay. I'll hear you out," I say.

Havander straightens as if a weight has lifted from his chest. "Thank you." He looks over his shoulder then back. "But first, we must go somewhere safe. This tale is dangerous told in unguarded places."

The stables recede behind us, the rugged warmth of the building swallowed by the rainforest and gloom of underground dusk. Ahead water chortles quietly. I wade through the thick ferns, following Havander.

The river appears from behind a stand of lemon

myrtle. The moss-covered bridge I saw earlier from the hill stretches across it. On the opposite bank tower stark, grey ruins.

Havander turns. His eyes glow green like a dog's in low light. "This is Ashnah Keep," he says. "Ancestral home to my kind. Or was. Once."

He crosses, heading for the broken building. His anklet catches the light as he moves.

I ignore a growing sense of foreboding. Not sure how clever it is to ignore my instincts, but it's too late to turn back now. My boots scuff quietly over the worn stones of the bridge. On the opposite side, dull, black-and-grey-flecked granite walls bare their teeth. Their surfaces are scorched, the edges ragged like broken ribs. Recessed in the centre panel, a huge charred timber door stands ajar. The details, carved in relief on its exterior face—exotic birds and Tasmanian tigers—can still be seen.

The forest around us has fallen silent, a hushed and almost apprehensive holding of breath. Havander beckons from the doorway, his chest now glowing blue. The light offers small comfort as I follow him into what was once a great hall.

The dank air inside the room clings to me, wet and heavy. Havander's illumination dances as he walks, chasing away some shadows and creating others. We skirt a large broken table circled by shattered stone chairs. Mouldering tapestries hang ragged from the slimy walls. He passes them without comment and leads us through another doorway at the far end.

The room beyond is smaller and in better repair. A

serviceable root-woven table and four chairs hold the centre of the room. A fire lamp hangs on a hook by a solid iron door standing closed on the right-side wall.

Havander stops. "Rigeander?" he calls.

The metal door creaks open. An old changer steps into the room, a bunch of keys clutched in one hand. He is dressed, like all the others, in grey robes.

"Havander? Is that you?"

"It is, and I've brought a guest."

"So the girl agreed to come?"

"Yes."

"Let's hope you are right about her then."

Rigeander swivels. The light shifts and the planes of his blue face are revealed. I stumble back a step, shocked at the brutal scars that disfigure his appearance—raised, rugged welts that buckle and pucker the lines of his nose and mouth.

"Don't look so scared, girl," says the changer, scratching his bald head. "I look like a monster, but I won't bite you."

I nod, uneasy. I check to see if he's wearing an anklet. He is.

"Reeva, this is Rigeander," says Havander. "He's my friend and the oldest of our kind here. He watches over the residents of Ashnah Keep."

"Residents?" I ask.

"Prisoners," says Rigeander.

Havander frowns. "Don't scare her. She's agreed to hear what we have to say."

The old changer chuckles and waves a crotchety hand. "Don't worry about me, girl. These last few hundred years being a slave have made me snappy." He leans in and then squints at Havander. "You didn't tell me she was pretty."

"I didn't tell her you were strange."

Rigeander grins and the years fall away from him. And while he does come off as weird, a gut feeling tells me he's okay.

"Well, she knows now," he says and winks at me. "Take a seat, Reeva, and make yourself at home. I'll get the tea on."

CHAPTER THIRTEEN

Rigeander shuffles around the room, boiling water and dolloping what he claims to be pepperberry and wild honey jam onto slabs of fresh bread. Havander sits opposite me at the small table, elbows held close. The lamplight trembles around us, closing the space in.

"We weren't always slaves, Reeva," begins Havander quietly. "Once changers stood as equals alongside the others, for like them, we are a wilder race too. They represent fire, earth, water and air, but we are the fifth element."

"Aether?" I ask. "You said those wilders were often forgotten."

Havander nods. "We are. Aether exists above the terrestrial sphere. We embody fluidity. We are the dreamers who see the potential for all futures."

Rigeander rests the food on the table. Three cups of lemon myrtle tea follow, their aroma curling deliciously.

The old changer eases into a chair and slurps a

mouthful. "Yes," he says. "But no good came from our visions. We saw and warned the others what humans would do if not educated. We prophesied the wholesale slaughter of whales, the decimation of forests, and invasive mining. When it all came to pass, our brothers and sisters said it was *our* fault, that we'd manipulated humanity to engineer the outcome. They declared it a rebellion, our fight to gain greater authority in the council and in the drafting of natural laws."

Rigeander takes a bite of bread and chews. Crumbs tumble to his chest. "But that wasn't the case."

"So the others enslaved you," I say, "to stop what they thought you were doing?"

"That was the claim." Havander frowns. "But in truth they feared change. We, being the very embodiment of it, make us their opponents."

"But that's stupid," I say. "The world is obviously in trouble. Humanity needs help."

Havander nods. "It's true."

"But if you guys are for saving the planet too, why are the changers topside cutting down the Elder Trees?" I ask.

"They're desperate," says Rigeander.

"For what?" I take a sip of my tea. The hot lemon flavour floods my mouth.

Havander looks up. Unspoken words pass between him and Rigeander.

"We can show you," says Rigeander. "But the truth isn't nearly as pretty as you."

The sadness in his voice hints at destinies failed and fates bound.

"Show me," I say.

Behind the iron door is a corridor that leads to a prison block. Havander and Rigeander guide me past a row of medieval-styled cells. No beds or comforts are afforded inside the small spaces, just a single blanket and a water bowl. In the fickle light I glimpse changers in some of the rooms, huddling tight to the rear corners. They mutter in guttural tones, their eyes wide and feral.

"What is this place?" I ask.

"Ashnah Keep Prison," says Rigeander. "This is where slaves are sent for terms of imprisonment. Their minds have been stripped away by wilder bracelets."

"They're driven mad as punishment?"

"Yes."

"Do they ever get their sanity back?"

"The bracelets can reverse the change, if the wilders choose to do it."

I glance into another cell. The emaciated slave locked inside is curled on the floor, shoulder bones protruding like dead branches. The control anklet on its leg though remains tight. My heart twists, appalled.

"Is this the place Dacien was talking about when we met, Havander?" I ask. "The prison you were sent to when you lost the human who damaged the Elder Tree?"

He looks away as if ashamed. "It was."

Horrified, I try and imagine him as mindless and locked away in a cell.

"This is sickening," I say. "Why are they kept like this?"

"They are being punished," says Rigeander. "I do what I can to make them comfortable, but if I give them anything more, I'd be sent to join them."

"Their treatment is the crime here," I growl.

"This is what the escaped changers are fighting for," says Havander. "Every one of them has someone they love in this place. They only want their kin released."

"I don't blame them." Cold rage smoulders in my belly. These poor changers are languishing here while the councillors sneer and sit in their regal chambers. I turn, lips pressed thin. "I don't need to see anymore."

"You'll support us then?" asks Havander.

Rigeander keeps his gaze fixed to the floor, as if afraid of my answer.

Their anklets gleam ominously.

"Someone has to stand for what's right, and this," I say, pointing at the cells, "is far from right. No one deserves to live like this."

My mind races. I want to help, but I have to be careful. My own position here is tenuous. I haven't forgotten the council's promise of a sunrise slaying.

"What are you thinking of doing?" asks Havander.

Considering the complex web of hatreds, there is only one thing I can do.

"I'm going to talk with Dacien. Maybe I can persuade him to help me."

"He won't," says Havander.

"Probably. But he's the only wilder in this place who

won't kill me outright for saying what I think about this. He'll listen first."

"And if he listens, you think you can sway his loyalty?"

"I don't know. But maybe I can get him to talk to his mother, and *he* can ask *her* to try and change the other councillor's minds. I'm willing to give it a go."

Havander and Rigeander share an uneasy glance.

"What about your father?" asks Havander.

I frown. "He'd want me to do the right thing."

"I'm worried what will happen if you speak with Dacien."

"Have you got any better ideas?"

"If we did, we'd already be free," replies Rigeander.

"Then this is our plan."

I turn and head for the exit, Havander and Rigeander in tow.

"Reeva?"

I stop. The new voice comes from the darkened cell to the right of me. It filters, weak and hoarse, through the rusted bars but I'd recognise it anywhere.

"Dad?"

"What's left of me ..."

I race to the cell, hands gripping the bars like vices. It's dark and I can't see anything inside. I spin, heart pounding like a hammer to an anvil.

"Is that my *father*?" I ask, trying to remain calm and failing. "Why is he in there?"

Rigeander retreats, hands raised. "The council brought this man here."

I grind my teeth. "They told me he was with your

healers!" The betrayal stings. "Get him out now. I'm taking him home."

"I don't dare," says Rigeander. "I'll be punished for freeing him without an anklet."

"What do you mean?" asks Havander. "Humans don't need anklets."

"You don't know? He is no longer human," says Rigeander. "He was bitten and is almost fully changed."

"He's been BITTEN?" I cry, incredulous.

Havander swings on Rigeander. "Why didn't you tell me?"

The old changer falls back another step. "Councillor Hestia herself put him in here. She forbade me to tell anyone."

"I never took you for a coward."

"I'm not, my friend," says Rigeander. "I'm a survivor."

Havander shakes his head. He pushes past me and approaches the cell door. The lamp he holds chases away the shadows and my stomach drops. My father— or what was once my father—sits huddled against the rear wall. He's barely recognisable. His skin is mottled blue and white and his steel-coloured hair has fallen away in patches. He crawls forward and clutches the iron bars, fingernails already turned to black claws.

"Turn him back," I plea.

"I can't reverse it," whispers Havander. "It's a change, not an ailment to be healed."

My heart sinks. "But why would your people bite him?"

Havander's hands tremble. "All I know is they would've been fighting for their lives that night."

"And that's an excuse?"

"No. Not at all."

Dad shifts. "Get me the hell out of here, Reeva," he growls.

The familiar tightening in my chest—the knee-jerk reaction to do what Dad wants, when he wants it done—has me turn on Rigeander. "You heard him," I snarl. "Open it."

"I can't. I'm sorry," he says.

Frustrated, I pound on the cell bars. The iron groans under the blows but doesn't yield. I'm not strong enough. But I have my power. I recall how Hestia broke the glass with her shield. Maybe I can burst the lock the same way. I draw on Dacien's lessons —focus, find and pull from a source. Pressure builds in my forehead. I squeeze my eyes shut. The scar on my arm burns. I sense the moisture in the bodies of the prisoners in the other cells. I gather it. There isn't much. I draw harder.

A hand gently touches my shoulder.

"Reeva," says Havander, gently. "Stop. You'll hurt them."

Guilt undoes me. I'm no better than a wilder for using these creatures. I open my eyes. A thin, weak looking screen of glittering droplets hangs suspended around us—a spherical shield. Cold silver fire licks my arm. I let the magic ease and the moisture swirls, returning to the prisoners. I can't save Dad like this.

Not at the cost of other, more helpless lives. I turn to my father.

But he isn't looking at me.

"Is that you, Havander," he asks, "or am I dreaming?"

The changer sighs. "Emmett, my old friend, it's been a long time."

Dad slumps against the wall. "Not long enough."

CHAPTER FOURTEEN

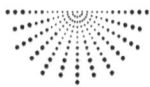

"How do you know my father?"

Havander runs a hand down his face. The lines around his mouth have deepened as if a weight he carries is suddenly all the heavier. In the cage opposite, Dad rests with his head against the bars.

"We met many years ago." Havander glances sideways at me. "The night your mother went missing."

My pulse hitches. "What do you know about that?"

Havander straightens. His robe tightens across his chest, highlighting his lean frame. "Your father was desperate. I found him in the forest hacking his way into the Elder Tree. Your mother had taken you and he was determined to get you back."

Dad acting the hero? I've only ever known the man hell bent on drinking himself to death.

"I don't believe you," I say.

"You should," says Rigeander. "Your father is the human Havander went to prison to protect."

"I willingly paid the price to help him," whispers Havander.

"Why didn't you tell me this before? How can I trust you now?"

Havander's mouth presses into a hard, flat line. "I was afraid. I realised who you were, but didn't know what kind of person you'd become. What if I told you and you betrayed me to the council? My next prison term would have been far longer than just a year."

He has a point. I swallow my anger.

"Well, tell me everything now then," I say. "You know you can trust me."

"I know." Havander frowns in his recall of another place and another time. "Your mother courted Emmett and fell pregnant," he says. "Your father, in love with her, was thrilled, but a hybrid child was not what she wanted. After she gave birth to you, she stole you away. Instead of admitting her mistake to the council and risking her own demise, your mother took you to Live Well and threw you in. She left you there, not knowing that the well was dry in that season and that you being stronger than a normal human child, had survived the fall."

My mother tried to kill me? I reel. What kind of woman would do that?

Then I remember she isn't a woman at all, she isn't human.

"I returned you to your father," continues Havander, "but I couldn't hide the damage to the Elder Tree. I told the council that the man who did it escaped me and I was sent to prison as punishment. The councillors at the time never learnt the truth."

I realise I'm only alive today *because* of Havander. I owe him more than I thought.

"Did my mother ever find out I was still alive?"

"She did, but by then it was too late."

"Why?" I ask.

"Your father had leverage over her."

"What leverage?"

"I told him of a crime she had committed that was far worse than just giving birth to you. She had seduced and tricked Emmett for her own gain. Wanting greater control over her abilities in order to secure a place on the council, your mother had bloodbound herself to Emmett."

"Bloodbound?"

"If a wilder lingers away too long from the underground forests that are their source of power, their magic fades and they become human. It is their only weakness."

So Neru had indeed told me the truth.

Havander scratches his ear. "But there is a way to circumvent the rule. If a wilder's blood is mingled with a human's, a bloodbind is formed, connecting the two life forces together. This prevents the wilder's loss of power and gifts the other a type of immortality. Neither can die while their bonded partner lives. Your mother used Emmett to secure her own unlimited power and left him heartbroken in the process."

The changer sighs. "A confirmed bloodbind would have meant both your father and your mother's execution. My kind accept such bonds and welcome the connections, but to the others, it's considered unclean."

"So my father is still connected to her?"

Havander shakes his head. "No. Our venom changes the genetic constitution of blood and dissolves bonds formed by other wilders. When Emmett has fully changed, he will be free of her. But, it also means he is in grave danger. She'll want him dead then to protect herself and she *will* be able to kill him."

The pieces of Havander's story clatter around my head like loose stones. They slip and fall into place. Suddenly Dad's attempted suicide takes on new meaning. He'd loved my mother and she'd hurt him long before I ever left to go to uni. And he'd wanted to die— tried to die—but couldn't. None of this had ever been my fault.

Another thought occurs. "So that means my mother is still alive? You know who she is?"

My father stirs. His cheeks are streaked with tears. I've never seen him cry. I'm used to the man made of granite with a temper that could melt mountains. I have spent my entire life loving him and fearing him in equal measure.

"I'm sorry I never told you, Reeva." Dad blinks and rubs his nose. "I loved her more than my own life, but she can't return it. She's incapable. Remember that when you meet her. Don't be taken in."

"Who is she?" I ask, almost fearing the answer.

My father reaches through the bars. I hesitate but then grasp his hand. He squeezes mine, his skin fevered against my palm.

"Hestia," he replies, "of the Fireborn Wilders. She's your mother."

My world has tilted sideways. How can Hestia be my mother? Dacien did say fire gives birth to water. God, that means he's my brother. Well, my half-brother at least. I'm not sure exactly how I feel about that.

Havander leads me away from the ruins. Rigeander has promised to watch over my father until I return. I hate the thought of Dad being left in that cage, but it's the safest place for him right now.

"Are you sure you want to do this, Reeva?" asks Havander.

"Yes. Forget Dacien. I'm going straight to Hestia and demand she lets him go."

"It's too dangerous, she'll do anything to protect herself."

"It may seem foolhardy, but if anything happens to me, Neru, at least, will start asking questions. He thinks I hold some kind of value. If she hurts me, Hestia will risk exposing her secrets."

I run my hand through my fringe. "If she refuses me, I'll threaten her. I'll tell the other councillors who my mother is and what she's done."

Havander chuckles quietly. "Like a bull at a gate. You are more your father's daughter, than your mother's."

"I'm starting to think that's not such a bad thing."

"It's not."

I steal a glance at the changer. "Why did you risk helping Dad all those years ago?"

Havander's smile turns grim. "Emmett loved you enough to fight for you. I saw a good man. That was enough for me."

"You recognised me in the forest the other night, didn't you? That's why you saved me?"

"Correct."

"Thank you," I whisper. "For both times you had my back."

Havander grasps my shoulder, the touch reassuring. "You're most welcome, Reeva."

CHAPTER FIFTEEN

Night has fallen across the valley as we take the front path into Hestia's home. Inside smells of jasmine and wattle. The lamps lining the corridor are lit, spilling puddles of light along the floor.

The door to my mother's office, just left of the main entrance, stands ajar. I pause before entering.

You can do this.

You have to do this.

I rap at the doorpost, three quick taps.

"Enter," says Hestia.

Havander touches my arm. "I'll be out here."

Inside, the room is a well-appointed affair. The walls are lined with cascading plants, their small pink flowers filling the space with a delicate perfume. Plush rugs soften my footsteps as I approach Hestia's desk, its Blackheart Sassafras top heavily grained and well-polished. Papers lie scattered in front of her, covered in writing I don't understand; letters resembling leaves and twisted roots.

Hestia, dressed in vivid blue house robes, a blue that highlights the bright red of her hair, sits behind it. Liander, lingers silent in the corner of the room.

"Reeva," says Hestia, elegant eyebrows lifted in mild surprise. She places her ink quill neatly in the pot sitting next to a stack of papers.

"Hestia," I say, coolly. I slip into a woven chair, balancing myself on the edge.

A small furrow buries itself on her brow. She smiles, almost too sweetly. "It's nice to see you," she says. "How is your training going with my son?"

Her son. The full-blooded wilder she thought worth keeping. The child she *didn't* want to kill.

"Slow," I say. "I've made some progress but still find it hard to control the magic."

Hestia nods. "It can be difficult for hybrids. Your humanity hinders your abilities. You are lucky to have powers at all. Most like yourself are not born with magic."

I clench the muscles in my cheeks. "Met a lot of hybrids have you?"

She smiles again. "No, but history tells us such things. But do not concern yourself. Whatever skills you can manage will be of great benefit to our cause."

Their cause.

"You mean the cause to keep your own lives just the way you like?"

Hestia's yellow eyes thin, just a millimetre. She half turns her head and nods to Liander. The woman gathers her grey slave robes and slips from the room.

My mother's gaze returns to me, a glare of brimstone clothed in silk. "Why are you here?"

I pluck a hair off my sleeve and smile, trying to put the exact same sweetness to it that she had in hers before—like mother, like daughter and all.

"I want to see my father."

Hestia relaxes. She sighs, pushes her chair back and stands. Circling the table, she gathers my hands in her own. Her touch, again, is almost too hot to bear. I tense.

"He is not well," she says. "And still needs to heal. You wouldn't want to jeopardise his recovery, would you? We will let you know when you can go to him."

I explore her features, ones that seem so completely alien to me. How can this woman be my mother? I feel no connection to her at all.

"You're lying," I say.

Red sparks trip down Hestia's forearms. A warning?

"How so?" she asks.

I lift my chin, hoping it makes me look defiant. "I know he's your prisoner. I'm here to ask you respectfully to release him. I'll take him home and care for him there."

My mother's nails dig into the back of my hands. "Have you seen him?"

"Yes."

"When?"

Not wanting Havander or Rigeander implicated, I invent a little lie of my own. "Just now. I snuck out and went for a walk by the river. I found your prison."

Hestia's top lip wrinkles. She believes me. "Well, then you know that man is not your father anymore."

"Blood is blood," I say. "He'll always be my dad."

A vein pulses in her throat. She's trying to decide how much I know, I'm sure of it.

"Look," I say. "I don't care what you think or what secrets you're trying to hide. I *will* be taking him home one way or another."

"Emmett belongs to us."

Hestia releases my hands. Embers trip between her fingers.

"I know who you are," I say, throwing caution to the wind.

Her jaws clench.

"Look," I continue. "Neither one of us wants anything to do with you. We just want to leave. Dad, once he has changed, can pass off as human and you'll be safe. I promise."

Hestia sneers. "This is bigger than you and Emmett. Can't you see that?" She closes her eyes and steadies her breath. Her voice softens. "Please, Reeva. I need your support on this."

She grasps my hand again. Her skin feels even hotter.

She's nervous, I'll bet.

"Tomorrow night is solstice," she continues, "and our powers are at their height. This is our best chance to round up the escaped changers. If you can hold off revealing your lineage, I'll ensure you get your freedom. Emmett is lost, and I am sorry for that, but in myself and Dacien, you'll find a family that loves you."

She's incapable ...

I pretend to consider her offer. Holding the silence, I let my shoulders slump as if defeated.

"I only want to protect Dad, but I think you are right. I barely recognise him. Maybe it *is* too late." I glance at her. "And I guess getting to know you better wouldn't be so terrible."

The lie comes so easily.

Hestia squeezes my hands. Her long red hair falls over my wrists as she bends to kiss my palm. My skin crawls at her touch.

"I would like to know you better also. Thank you, Reeva," she says, her relief palpable. "You've made a wise choice."

Yes, I have.

Havander steps in beside me as I leave the office. "You can't mean to abandon Emmett?"

"Of course not," I reply. "But I didn't want her throwing me in there with him."

"What now then?"

"I need to find Dacien."

The changer's nose wrinkles. "He'll be in the stables, but he is his mother's son. He won't betray the council."

"I don't need him to help us."

"What are you going to do?"

"Be a very mean big sister," I say.

CHAPTER SIXTEEN

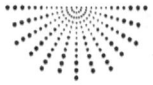

The shadowed forest resounds with the voices of nocturnal insects. Lights wink from within the stable building, bleeding through the woven root walls and across the lush greenery. The clipped ring of steel—the jangle of bridle bits and stirrups—breaks the evening.

Doubt fills me. What if I fail here?

"I'll find Dacien," I say as we pause by the main stable entrance. "You go and saddle Echo up. You know how to do that?"

"I do," replies Havander.

"Good. We'll need to get out quick, so don't waste time."

"What if someone queries me?"

I wind my fingers around the bottom of my ponytail. "Tell them you've been told to adjust the gear."

Havander's fingers worry at the edge of his grey sleeve. He's hesitant.

"You've got this," I say.

The changer smiles and for a moment he looks less a slave. "As do you."

~

Inside the stable is a bustle of industry. People scurry about sorting equipment and checking mounts over. A harried-looking, silver-eyed groom thrusts a saddle and bridle into Havander's arms. He points to Echo. "Get that gear sized to fit that horse."

Havander throws me a sly grin, clutches the equipment to his chest and heads away.

A good start. We may just pull this off.

I stalk past neat lines of stalls and into the work area at the rear of the building. Rows of racks fill the space, each stacked with piles of armour. I find Dacien sitting on a stool by a messy bench, weaving from buckets of water. His cheeks are flushed as if he has been at the job for some time. I pause and take in the look of him—his blue eyes and the fall of jet-black hair that mirrors my own in colour.

It feels weird knowing he's my brother.

"Dacien!" I call.

He pauses, silver threads glistening between his fingers. Half a breastplate sits in his lap. His smile seems genuine and for a moment, I feel guilty for what I'm about to do.

"Reeva! Where's Havander? He should be with you."

"He's helping with the horses. I thought I'd see how you're going. Your mum says we'll be heading topside tomorrow night."

Dacien nods. "Not long now." He lifts his fingers and spreads the threads to show me. They dance in the light. "You want to help me here?"

"I don't think I'm up to the task, sorry." I pick up a helmet from a stack on the table and turn it over. The surface feels almost like the fabric of my dress had been, but sturdier—more rubber-like. *Why not iron?*

"Water-wrought armour isn't as strong as iron," he says, somehow anticipating my thoughts, "but it's better because it is lighter for the horses to carry."

"Clever."

Dacien points to his bucket. "You should give it a go. Make something."

I rub my wrist. "I'll pass."

He smiles. "Practice makes perfect."

"In my case, I think perfection is unattainable."

I take a seat next to him and he starts to weave again. I glance at his bracelet. The silence deepens between us.

"Is everything all right?" he asks.

Nothing is all right, but where do I start?

"I've been thinking about families," I say, deciding on my course of action. "Do you have any siblings?"

My brother laughs. "No. My mother never sought another mate after my father died."

"Who was your father?"

Dacien smiles as if the memories he holds are fond ones. "Calix Airborn. An artisan. He was much older than my mother and passed on when I was quite young."

So in a way, we both grew up alone.

It's tenuous but, none-the-less, a thread of connection I have with my brother.

"I'm sorry to hear that. Do you wish you had a brother or a sister?"

"Why all the questions, Reeva?"

I pick up a loose strand of hay from the ground. "I'm just interested. Growing up for me was lonely. And now, worried about my dad, the support of a sibling who could help share that burden sounds oh-so-appealing."

Dacien severs the threads he is working with and starts on another section.

"I understand," he says. "But for me, I've always had my mother. Hestia is strong and steady."

"You're lucky to have a mum who's there for you," I say, swallowing back a sudden wave of bitterness.

"You never know," he replies, "maybe your mother had other children. They could be in this very city."

My heartbeat quickens and my palms grow sweaty. This is my opening …

"Actually," I say. "She did have another child."

Dacien stops, stormy eyes meeting mine. His bracelet catches the light.

"A son," I continue. "But he isn't a hybrid."

Dacien's eyebrows furrow. "How do you know this?"

"I worked it out."

"How?"

I lean in. "My dad," I whisper. "I've seen him. He told me who my mother is—who my brother is."

Dacien drops the threads of his magic. The breastplate falls to the bench. Incomplete, it breaks apart back into the water it was woven from. Rivulets of moisture soak the ground.

"Who are they?"

He doesn't know the truth.

"We have to tell the council," he says.

He definitely doesn't know the truth.

I take a breath. I don't want to hurt him. I don't want my brother to hate me when he hears what I have to say.

"Hestia is my mother." I try to announce it softly as if that will ease the gut-punch of such a statement. "Making *you* my brother—well, half-brother."

Dacien shakes his head once as if trying to process the words.

"You can't be serious?"

"I'm sorry. It's the truth."

He grips the bench as if to anchor himself. "Even after she invited you into our home, you're branding my mother a traitor?"

"I'm not planning on telling anyone. I just want my father and to get out of here. I need your help to escape."

Dacien scowls. "I won't help you escape! But I'll ensure your lies go no further than here." His voice rises. "Guards!"

Two wilders appear from nowhere.

"Gag her and take her to Ashnah Keep," orders Dacien.

"There's no need for this," I say.

Anger has turned my brother ugly. "Yes, there is."

"Then don't expect an apology."

"For what?"

I snatch for my brother's control bracelet. My fingers close around the metal and I pull. It doesn't come away at first, catching on his sleeve. We struggle and then it slips neatly into my hand. I leap to my feet and swivel, finding the first guard already at my back. My fist connects with his chin and a high-kick floors the other man standing behind him.

Dacien's frustrated growl follows me as I sprint for the exit.

Havander waits for me, already mounted on Echo.

"Head for the keep," I yell as he hauls me into the saddle behind him.

The changer urgently presses his heels to Echo's side. The mare, eager for a run, leaps for the exit. Her hooves clatter on the flagstones and then pound soft earth as we clear the stables.

Cries follow us, but Echo is the wind. She races low and fast towards the ruins. Dacien's bracelet is a cold, hard presence in my hand.

I grasp it tighter.

It's the only hope I have.

CHAPTER SEVENTEEN

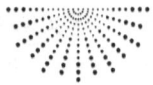

Rigeander waits by the mouldering bridge, eyes wide as we clatter past in a torrent of hoof beats and horse-flesh. Echo snorts and pulls up at Havander's command, stopping just short of the keep's entry. The changer slips from the saddle and helps me down.

"This was your plan?" Havander asks, incredulous.

Rigeander trots closer. "How did you get a bracelet?" he asks, eyes wide.

"It's Dacien's," I say. "I'm going to use it to set you all free."

From the distance, shouts bleed through the forest. My brother and more guards, no doubt. I slip the bracelet on, its cold circumference pinching my wrist.

"Only elemental wilders can control those things," says Havander. "I'm not sure if you'll be able to."

"I have to try." I kneel by Havander's leg, tap the bracelet and wake the anklet. Placing my hands around its glowing circumference, I close my eyes.

Magic thrums through the metal. It's complex and I

understand it no further than recognising it's a weave of the four physical elements.

Well, if I can detect them, maybe I can separate them—use a shield as a tool.

Just like shattering a glass.

I suck in a breath and pray this works.

I pull moisture from the river, the easy source that harms no living thing. Pain wakens, and with it power, rippling under my skin like mercury. It travels to the weak point on my arm.

When I open my eyes, silver light spills from my scar and across the anklet. I bite against the burn and manage to tighten the magic into a small, flat shield and worm it in between the anklet and Havander's skin. The metal repulses the invasion, flaring into a lasso of fire. Havander cries out and Rigeander grasps his friend's shoulder. Healing light pours from the old changer's fingers and Havander's pained grimace eases.

"Keep going, Reeva," says Rigeander, his scarred face determined.

Sweat beads on my forehead. I shove harder against the anklet, coaxing the slippery threads of my magic into the thin gap between it and the changer's skin. The shield slips through in a shower of sparks and somehow melds with the water threads already woven through the metal. I focus and imagine forcing the molecules apart. Then something clicks inside of me, a recognition of power centred in my heart and sluicing through my blood, and for the first time, I realise I am in control of the magic.

Seizing the advantage, I bend my shield, causing it to bulge.

More shouts, louder now, come from the forest. I ignore them.

Grow, shield, grow!

The anklet shatters in a whine of distressed steel. Splinters nick my palm. I snatch my hand away.

It worked!

Havander heaves. His thin chest draws air like he hasn't breathed deep in ages.

Rigeander releases him. "Are you all right?"

"I … will be," replies Havander. "Now your turn. Brace yourself."

I clasp the next anklet. It still hurts, but the power comes easier this time. I wedge the shield between the metal and Rigeander's skin. His scarred face tightens as he grits his teeth, but he doesn't cry out. Then his shackle shears apart also.

Dacien was right. Practice does make perfect.

I get to my feet, rubbing at the cold throb centred on my scar. "We need to release the others."

Rigeander takes my hand and with his healing light heals the small cuts on it. Faint red marks are branded reciprocally on his own hands, the cost for his kindness.

"Thank you." His voice cracks. "I've been bound to that anklet for far too long."

I squeeze his fingers. "We still have to make it out of here."

The old changer nods. "You're right. Come on."

Twenty slaves are locked in the prisons. Rigeander

shuffles ahead of me, opening doors. I move from cell to cell, heart sinking as the pitiful creatures shrink away from me. I approach them as gently as I can. One by one I touch their anklets and release them from the binding. My scar aches, but the outcome is worth the pain. With magical influence removed, sanity returns quickly to the liberated changers.

Dad's cell is last. I approach and peer in. He stands at the centre of the small, simple room, arms hanging by his sides and edges, fluttering uncertainly. Nothing of the body he once had remains. But he seems stronger for it somehow; clear-eyed and sober for the first time I can remember.

Rigeander leans in close to my ear. "His ability to morph has manifested. It will be chaotic with him being new to the skill, but he'll be able to shift if needed."

I glance at him. "That'll come in useful."

I open the cell door and step in. "You ready to go, Dad?"

My father shakes his head. "I don't deserve this."

"It's okay. We will make the changes work. I'll look after you."

He points to his body. "I don't mean the physical change. I mean I don't deserve your help. Leave me here. I'll slow the wilders up a bit."

The freed changers mill in the corridor behind me. We don't have time for this.

"Are you asking me to watch you try and kill yourself again?" I bark.

My father's mouth opens then snaps shut. It's like

he'd never before considered that his actions had consequences for me.

"I never meant for you to see that."

"Well, I did. Now get your shit together. We need to go."

I've never been brave enough to speak like that to him before. But something has dislodged in me, like a brick in the wall that stifles my courage, has weakened.

"And don't ever threaten to sacrifice yourself again," I say.

He surges forward and pulls me into a rough hug.

"Never, Reeva," he whispers. "Never again. I'm sorry."

I fiercely hug him back.

The forest streams by in a blur of green and grey. The memory of a real sky, instead of the stone overhead, draws me on. We are so close.

I cling to Echo's reins and huddle low to her neck. The air whistles cold by my ears. Behind me follow the calls of angry wilders.

Catch us if you can.

Twenty-three blue horses race alongside me, the changers and my father, who after a few false starts managed to consolidate the form. Ahead loom the ruins of Live Well. Just beyond them is the hill, and the exit offered by the Elder Tree.

We pass the broken terraces and the well. Dad gallops to my left, his sapphire mane rippling like torn streamers. Havander keeps pace on my right, racing neck and neck with Echo.

A splinter of opaque-white light breaches the vegetation ahead.

"Beware the air wilder," snorts Havander.

He veers left and the herd follows him, heads tossing and nostrils wide as they crash through the undergrowth. The white light cracks through the glade again and catches one changer around the neck. He rears backwards with an equine scream, hooves cleaving the air. Echo carries me on. The shrill yell of the wilder's victory trails in my wake.

Echo huffs as she scales the hill. Foam slicks her neck but, thoroughbred to the core, she grinds the incline with determination. One step follows the next —one hell of a mare—she continues until the towering presence of the Elder Tree's root system materialises ahead.

Havander changes shape, mid-step. One moment a horse, humanoid the next, he slams a hand against the wall and the tree's roots retreat, slithering back to reveal an entrance larger than I remember. The herd streams in. I drag Echo to a halt by Havander's side. She chomps at the bit and sidles, agitated. I run a hand down her soaked neck.

"Almost there, girl," I say.

More ribbons of power snap through the forest—white, silver, red, and gold.

"Quickly," urges Havander. He slaps a hand on Echo's rump and she surges into the room's embrace with a clatter of steel-shod hooves.

I rein her in and turn in the saddle. "You too."

But Havander lurches upright, wide-eyed and trembling in the doorway. His edges quaver as if his form is stuck halfway between one shape and another. Then a coil of opaque-white power erupts, crackling and sizzling, through the centre of his chest. The changer's eyes drop to the front of his robes. He shudders sickeningly as the magic retreats leaving a fist-sized hole where a human's heart would be.

Behind him, fifty metres away, stands a wilder I recognise. It's Aria, the soldier-woman I saw in the council chambers on my first day here. She stands, teeth bared and hands blazing.

"No!" I kick Echo and the mare swivels. I drag Havander up and onto the saddle, his breaths a wet gurgle in this throat. The entrance behind us contracts, darkness dropping like a curtain.

No. No. No. Please hold on, Havander.

With heart pounding, I muscle Echo into a gallop. Across the room, the passage is open, leading topside. Rigeander, now humanoid, gestures urgently. We race past him, leaving the underground to enter a forest filled with a wash of watery winter sunlight.

CHAPTER EIGHTEEN

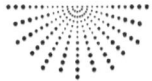

The Elder Tree closes behind us. Ahead, the changers circle the clearing, blue hides gleaming in the light.

Rigeander places a hand on Havander's brow and frowns. "A mortal wound. If I absorb this damage alone to heal him, it will kill me," he says. "A healing circle can do it, but we can't stop here. The wilders are still coming for us."

I nod. "To our place then. It isn't far. Head west until you see the gate with the name *Tarina* on it. You guys fly. I'll carry Havander and meet you there."

"No," nickers Dad. "We stick together."

"Okay," I say. "But let's move quickly."

Rigeander's chest glows momentarily as he shifts into his stallion form. He calls to the others and they crowd closer. My father takes the lead, heading for the highway and home. I check on Havander. His skin is clammy, but a pulse still flutters at his neck. He's unconscious but alive. I pull him closer.

"Don't give up on me," I whisper.

The forest peels away on each side of us. A pall of expectation hangs in the atmosphere. It's as if the living world holds its breath, waiting to see what happens.

A blast of gold electricity splinters suddenly past my shoulder and scorches a bush to my right. Echo swerves, and I slip sideways in the saddle. I right myself and grip the reins with one hand and steady Havander with the other. The attacking wilder flits away, pale hair fanning around her shoulders as she goes. I glimpse the earth-forged weapon she carries, a hammer of gathered rocks, dirt, and the binding light of her magic.

Another blast comes from the left, this time metallic-red—power that carries heat. Echo veers again. Ahead, the freed changers, all except Dad, switch into the familiar half-humanoid, half-animal creatures armed with black claws. They circle back and surround me, facing outwards. Low growls ripple their throats.

Echo skids to a stop, nostrils wide with panic. Dad sidles up next to me, his flank pressed to Echo's.

"Settle, girl," he nickers into her ear. She may not recognise his face but she knows his voice, and her anxious jostling eases.

Dacien appears from the forest, gaze dark as a thunderstorm. His active power flickers, encasing both fists. Ten other guards, a mix of elementals, emerge also to encircle us. Together, they are both beautiful and terrifying.

The changers gather closer, chittering.

Dacien's chin lifts, all arrogance like our mother. "You claim to be family but defend our enemies?"

"You don't believe I'm your sister, so why do you care?" I ask.

His nose wrinkles. "Because, either way, you're on the wrong side. You have wilder blood in your veins."

"And a human's compassion," I assert.

His distain reflects in the hard, cold set of his mouth.

"Reeva owes you nothing, boy," says Dad coming to my rescue. "She's where she should be, standing by those who need her most."

"Go home, Dacien," I say. "I've made my choice."

My brother's gleaming fists flare. The ferns around him wilt as moisture gathers on his fingertips and freezes to form a long spear of ice. "I won't let you betray us."

"Try and stop me then!" I raise my scarred arm and my own power burgeons to life. The trees offer me what I need. I mould a translucent, spherical shield large enough to encompass all the changers and myself.

"I don't want to fight you, Dacien," I say. "But I will protect these people."

My brother snarls and throws the spear. The weapon glances off my barrier and shatters on the ground.

"Tomorrow night at the solstice," he says. "We'll be backed by the full force of our power. No shield will help you then."

Before I can answer, an air wilder to the left screams. He flails then topples, disappearing into the undergrowth. The others shift on their feet, magic-forged weapons clutched uselessly in their hands.

There is no sign of the attacker. Another blood-curdling cry and a fire wilder is dragged away. The remaining guards panic and scatter.

My brother dips into a defensive half-crouch.

"This ends tomorrow," he says.

Then he is gone before I can even blink, a rustle of grasses the only thing marking his passage. But other movement soon follows in his wake. My adrenaline spikes as a group of twelve blue tiger snakes, the size of crocodiles, slither from the forest.

I reinforce my shield, ready to defend against these new attackers.

But instead, they halt.

"They're gone," hisses one serpent.

The reptiles glow and their forms change. The largest becomes a burly, human-looking man—chestnut hair, almost-white eyes, ruddy skin and a flat nose.

"Free changers," breathes Rigeander excitedly.

"It's bloody Dan Anderson," mutters Dad.

Our neighbour shakes his head. "You're welcome, Emmett," he says.

So the Andersons are changers.

Are there *any* humans in this district?

Dan is gentle as he eases the reins from my still-tightened grip. "Here, Reeva. Let me help your friend."

I ease Havander into my neighbour's care. He lays him out on the mossy ground. Around us, the other changers gather silently. I dismount and kneel, my lap sodden with blood.

"He's gone," whispers Dan, and my heart lurches.

"You're sure?"

Dan nods, once. My bottom lip trembles. Havander's pale gaze is fixed to some distant horizon that only the dead can see.

"Havander," I whisper, grief, helplessness, and rage warring within me. It's not fair. My chin drops to my chest as a sob chokes my throat. Tears drip off my chin.

Rigeander kneels next to me. His scars, etched with bone-deep sorrow, seem all the more prominent in the light of day.

"I'm sorry," I say. "I didn't … I couldn't … I could have shielded him but I wasn't watching."

The admission of failure undoes me. I can't seem to breathe in enough air.

"You didn't fail him, Reeva," whispers Rigeander. He pulls my chin around to face him. "He died *free* because of you. You gave him that."

"He's dead. I gave him that too."

"No one is ever truly dead," says the old changer. "Let me show you."

Rigeander helps me to my feet and draws me away to the side.

One by one, Havander's kin circle his corpse and they begin to sing. The melody, born from their collective voices, spirals off into the sky—music that speaks of sunlight, starlight, and the mutable nature of change.

Havander's corpse blurs. His body morphs, stretching up, growing taller and taller. Roots grow from his back and dig deep into the damp, rich earth. His arms become branches, rising up into the topmost part of the forest's canopy, and his legs spiral together to become a thick wooded trunk draped in ragged bark.

A eucalyptus tree—a living part of the forest.

And as the breeze catches his leaves, I swear I hear the words—

Thank you, Reeva.

CHAPTER NINETEEN

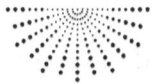

Dan and Rigeander, much to my father's disappointment, decided it would be best to head to the Anderson farm instead of home—a more defensible position than our place, apparently. Having only ever had occasion before to scowl over the fence, this is the first time I've ever been inside Dan's house. It's quite homey here. The kitchen is warm and comfortable with timber panelled walls and floral-patterned linoleum floors. A filled firewood box sits next to a wood stove in one corner. Heat from the open grate fills the room, easing away the winter's chill.

My father has morphed into his human form, looking once again like he used to. He leans on the scuffed timber island bench and runs a hand through his hair.

"How's it that you're a bloody changer, Anderson?" he asks.

Dan, also looking every bit a human, sits at the table

next to a blue-skinned Rigeander. My neighbour curls his hand around a steaming cup of tea.

"I was born one." He takes a sip. "I escaped from The Styx as a teenager, fifty years ago—before they fitted an anklet on me. I've hidden in plain sight ever since. This property is a sanctuary for any others that manage to win free. Not that it's been many over the years. The wilders tend to keep their property close."

My estimation of Dan rises. Suddenly he isn't the bastard-of-a-neighbour my dad hates; he is a man with a moral core.

"Was it your lot that bit me the other night?" asks Dad.

Dan chews his bottom lip. His attention flicks to me and then away. "Not any of my crew. We were in the forest trying to help the ten who escaped. But they got to you before we did. You were covered in Reeva's blood and smelt like a wilder to them. I'm sorry."

"So, this is all my fault?" I ask.

Dad squeezes my arm, pressing on an old bruise from Havander's training. I swallow the sudden surge of grief at the subtle reminder of my lost friend.

"You got us out of the car," says Dad, "and their bites counteracted the bloodbind your mother forced on me. I'm thankful for what's happened. I now get to live and die on my own terms."

I realise he's right. It's a cup of coffee in front of him rather than vodka, and his hands have lost their tremble. Emmett Castor is no longer the suicidal drunk. He's a man looking to the future.

Maybe I should be too.

"What now?" asks Rigeander. "We have sanctuary for tonight, but tomorrow they'll be on the doorstep."

I nod. "They are well provisioned too. At least a hundred horses and gear prepped."

Dan smirks. "The fifty they stole from us won't matter," he says.

"Why?" I ask.

"Well," he says. "In the same way Emmett was bloodbound to your mother, our animals are all bound to us. The horses they took won't ride against us."

I grin. "That's a good start."

"But it's not enough to stop them," says Dad.

Rigeander coughs. "It's been a long time, but I fought wilders back in the day. I have some suggestions that may help."

"We'd be happy for the advice," says Dan.

Rigeander smiles crookedly. "How are we for numbers then?"

"There's thirty of us," says Dan. "And Galen Mayer will stand with us too."

My ears prick up at Galen's name.

"The constable?" asks Dad.

"Yes," says Dan. "He has no love for wilders."

"He knows about them?" I ask, not sure if that's a good or a bad thing.

Dan smiles, "Let's just say, he's had personal experience in dealing with them before."

A bad thing then.

"Haven't we all," says Dad. He shrugs. "A cop will be useful, I guess. But even so, we're short on people."

"It'll have to be enough," says Rigeander. He presses

both palms to the tabletop. "The good thing is, we don't need any weapons other than the skills we already have. Those snake forms you used earlier, Dan, are well suited to a fight in the forest terrain. We'll need to think about some kind of armour to protect us though."

I shove away the memory of Havander, standing unprotected, with power punched through his chest.

"I may be able to help," I say. "I watched Dacien build armour. It might not be pretty, but I can try to make something."

"The wilders will bring more than enough 'pretty' to the fight," says Rigeander. "We just need it to be tough and serviceable if you can manage it."

"I'll give it a go," I say.

"And I'll ring Galen and get him to come over," says Dan. "He won't mind a late call for this."

Rigeander nods. "Emmett and I will brief the others." He smiles at each of us in turn. "The time is ripe for a revolution."

His words resonate.

There's change in the wind.

Dan has lent his machinery shed for me to work in. The cavernous space smells like tractor engine oil, but it's neat and tidy. I sit at the stainless-steel bench fixed along the rear wall. Shelves span above me, heavy with machine parts and old boxes with faded labels.

I keep trying, but creating armour is hard. I wish I'd

paid more attention when my brother was making it. To be fair though, I had other things on my mind at the time. I concentrate again on the bowl of water in front of me. With focus, the familiar sting of activated power crawls along my scar. How did it look again when Dacien had woven his magic? I hold my hand out in front of me and imagine twisting it. The elements respond.

My heart leaps. It kind of looks right. The threads coiling in my palms are not nearly as delicate as my brother's had been but they'll work. Mentally, I outline an armour design that would suit a snake—interlocking scales to allow for movement. Common sense guides me. I'll forge articulated sections to cover the back and sides and another to protect the belly.

I gather the filaments and ball them together. With my thumbs, I smooth the first of the scales. It gleams an imperfect blue-silver. When it's finished, I place it on the bench where it promptly disintegrates back into liquid.

"Dammit," I curse, punching the bench in frustration.

A footstep scuffs the concrete floor behind me.

"That's not the way to do it."

I swivel on my chair. Galen is dressed in jeans, sneakers and a black Led Zeppelin T-shirt. He looks different out of uniform—slighter and less imposing. The shed's fluorescent lights catch in his hair like slivers of chrome.

My heart flutters like it used to in school. That weird *I really like him* flutter.

I ignore it and brush a loose strand of hair over my ear.

"What would you know about it?" I ask.

"More than you think," he replies, smiling.

A smile to die for.

He walks over and leans on the bench, the scent of his aftershave closing around me.

"You need to gather the element, twist it with your power and then mould it," he says. "When you finish though, you need to bind the ends of the threads or it all falls apart."

"Bind them?"

"Yes, kind of like tying a knot into a piece of string."

"Okay."

I sigh and try again. The threads come easily but are slippery to manage. I eventually get a granny knot in the end. This time the scale, although slightly misshapen, remains intact. I place it down.

"Not bad for a newbie," says Galen.

"Thanks. I only have thousands more to go."

Galen chuckles. "You need to think bigger. Don't mould a single scale, forge a whole sheet and then split and shape it. It's much faster."

"How do you know about this stuff?" I ask. "Dan mentioned you knew something about wilders."

"I have experience with their type of power."

I push the bucket of water closer to him. "You should be making this stuff then."

Galen shoves his hands into his pockets, as if he wants to hide them. "I can't. Not anymore."

"Anymore?"

Galen's lips twist into a grim smile. "Let's just say I miss the forests of my childhood home."

Suddenly I feel awkward, as if I've pried into business he may not want to talk about.

But then, fragments of a conversation with Havander push at my memory—

... If they linger away too long ... their magic fades and they become human ...

The pieces fall into place. "You're a wilder?"

Galen looks down. His hands press deeper into his pockets. "I was, once. Not anymore."

His features remind me of Councillor Cephos. "Earth?" I ask.

"Yes."

"Why aren't you one now?"

Galen picks up the scale. He turns it over. "Because a long time ago I tried to free a friend—a changer who saved my life." He frowns. "I was discovered and banished. Without being bloodbound to a human, I lost my powers and now here I am."

"What happened to your friend?"

"I heard she died in Ashnah Keep."

Pity resolves in my stomach.

Galen takes my hand—the first time he's ever touched me. The night air has cooled his skin, but I'm sure mine feels sweaty. He places the armour scale in my palm. "Dan told me you've lost a friend recently too."

Havander. My work had momentarily allowed me to forget.

"Yeah," I whisper.

"Tomorrow, then," says Galen. "We'll honour their memories."

His words, so sincere, raise goosebumps along my arms. I gently pull my hand away from his. "You're coming with us even though you're powerless?"

"Why live if you have nothing worth dying for?"

I think on my own life. What have I been living for? What would I die for?

Freedom. Family. Friends.

"That's a good point," I say.

"I'm a good human," he replies, laughing. He pulls over a spare stool and sits next to me at the bench. "We don't have much time. I'll guide you as you work."

I can't say I'm disappointed.

CHAPTER TWENTY

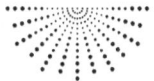

An overcast morning filters in through a gap in the curtains hanging across the bedroom's single window. The grey light brings with it the harder touch of winter. I groan against the cold and pull my pillow over my head. My whole body aches as if I've been through a wringer. My scar especially hurts. The night of work behind me has turned it into a white-hot line of pain that runs from wrist to elbow.

Outside, distant voices call to each other. The loudest are Dad and Dan, having a heated disagreement about how to best sharpen axes. I sigh, some things never change. I push the pillow away and get up. My feet meet cool jarrah floorboards. God, even my toes hurt. I sit and look around the room. It was late when Dan directed me here last night and I barely remember falling into bed. But in the daylight, I find the space pleasant. It's big and airy, the white walls contrasting nicely with the floor. A dark wardrobe sits next to the double bed holding the centre of the room. At the bed's base, a green crocheted blanket, looking like it came from the local Country Women's Association, lies next to a fluffy grey towel.

Just inside the door sits a wicker basket. I limp over and find toiletries and clean clothes inside. They must have been slipped into the room after I went to bed. I'm thankful for the care and consideration.

I take the basket and towel. The corridor outside is empty and I find the bathroom on the right. Inside the mirror is fogged and the faint smell of Galen's after-shave lingers. I draw the scent in, a mix of cedarwood and clary sage. I'd enjoyed spending time with him last night. His easy conversation made the work go quickly. After a bit, I hadn't even felt awkward anymore. It was like hanging out with a friend … albeit a drop-dead gorgeous one.

I shake my head. I really need to stop thinking about him like that.

"Dammit, Reeva," I hiss to myself. "Bigger things are at stake right now."

Angry with myself, I lean in and turn the shower on. I strip and step in, hoping there is still enough hot water left.

Heat sluices across my shoulders, working at the stiffness and the pain. I lean my forehead against the cold tiles and let myself drift. So much has changed in the last couple of days, and I've barely had time to process it. The shift in Dad's personality, the existence of magic, changers and wilders. I have a mother and a brother and I've both gained and lost friendships.

What all this means, I don't know. But one thing is certain. My world has irrevocably transformed.

And I suspect, so have I.

Twenty minutes later, I'm clean and ready to face the world. I tie my damp hair into a loose ponytail, shrug on a jacket and grab a piece of cold toast from the kitchen table. Outside, weak sunlight has broken through the cloudbank, rendering the day both bright and cool. I survey the farm from the rail of the house's wide, wrap-around verandah. Various sheds circle out in a fan shape from the main house. The machinery shed is the largest of the structures. The smallest is much older with rusted tin walls and looks to be the granary. To the left stands the stables, their oiled timber planks and carved sandstone block walls well-maintained but the lack of animals within is an ominous reminder of the fight ahead. Past the stables is a railed horse yard and beyond that, the wild North Styx Forest Reserve.

"Morning, Reeva," says a familiar voice.

Rigeander, dressed in a flannelette shirt and jeans is only recognisable by his scars, and the inflection of his accent. This morning he's adopted the human form of an elderly, grey-haired man. Standing by the machinery shed he beckons me over.

"Not a bad job." He points to the pile of water-wrought body armour stacked just inside the massive open doors—long, articulated cylinders, blue-silver in colour.

Galen had sat with me until just before dawn; guiding me on how to weave the sheets of fabric, mould and make them iron hard. The finished product lacks precision, shine, and ornament but are what Rigeander asked for—serviceable. Next to the pile lie two other suits of smaller human-shaped armour, one for Galen and one for me.

I squint against the sun. "I just hope they'll make a difference."

"They will," says Rigeander. "You've given us a fighting chance."

Dad walks around the corner of the shed, an axe in each hand. The newly sharpened edges gleam bright silver.

"More than a bloody fighting chance, I reckon." Dad grins like a shark. "My girl has given us the key to taking their kingdom." He holds up the axes. "And if the bastards have changed the locks, we'll cut down their front door."

I don't want to see any more destruction, but still, a surge of pride fills me. Who is this man that wears my dad's face? I barely recognise him. He's strong and confident. He has purpose and most of all he is proud of something I did.

I bask in the warmth of his approval, but am afraid to linger too long. It wouldn't do to get too used to it, just in case he changes his mind again.

I give him a lopsided grin. "Are we ready?"

Dad nods. "We just need to get fitted out."

I glance at the stacked armour. "But we don't need it until tonight, right?"

Dad shakes his head. "There's been some movement

in the forest this morning. Galen's just headed out to scout. We should be ready in case it's bad news."

Anxiety ripples through me. Hestia said they would attack at night. We should have had all day to prepare.

My father loses his smile and my heart sinks with it. He has sensed my weakness. I'm sure of it. I can already hear his rebuke—

Don't be so bloody dramatic ...

The glow from his previous comment fades.

"Reeva," he says, in a way I've never heard him speak before—a tone both soft and hard. "Find the part of yourself that's angry, the part of you that wants to defend what you love. These wilders don't understand such things. Passions and tempers. The human elements. These are what'll see us win. You can do this. I know you can."

I take a deep breath and focus on the strength that lies beneath my fear. I wipe my hands down my jeans and nod. "I got this, Dad," I say.

And I do, until Galen stumbles around the side of the shed, blood streaming from a gash in his forehead.

No!

"They're coming," he says, slumping into Rigeander's arms.

"Dan," bellows Dad. "Get the others. The bastards are on their way."

Changers stream in from all directions, their everyday clothing melding with skin as their humanoid forms shift into those of giant snakes. Dad fits the body armour to each one. The fit is far from perfect and the moving pieces scrape as the serpents slither away, past the horse yards and towards the forest.

Dan, still human-shaped, stalks up. "What happened?"

"They saw Galen," says Dad.

Rigeander lays the police officer on the ground and Dan kneels next to him. With glowing fingertips, he touches the jagged wound on Galen's head. As the ex-wilder's flesh knits, a new faint scar is born on Dan's own forehead.

Galen's eyes flutter open.

Both relieved he's okay and angry he let himself get hurt, I give Galen no quarter. I grab his armour and toss it on his chest. "Come on. Get up and get ready."

CHAPTER TWENTY-ONE

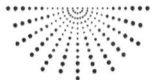

Thirty serpents slide ahead of us, rasping across the forest floor. Galen stalks by my side. His brow is creased and his shoulders are bowed, but dressed in his armour, his frame is otherwise cut into sharp, clean lines. He almost looks like the wilder he once was, a vision from a fairy tale.

"Are you ready for this, Reeva?" he asks, voice pitched low. "Good people will die today."

A chill races down my spine. I recall Havander lying cold and still.

"Good people have already died," I reply. "Ready or not, this needs to happen."

"I'm not sure I'm ready." He glances at me. "I may face old friends and family today."

For the first time I realise what it means for him to be taking the side of the changers—for him to stand against his own people.

"You can still change your mind," I whisper.

His smile holds no warmth. "No. It's time I made a stand."

"You don't have to do this."

Galen blinks and straightens. The lines of his face smooth and his gaze clears as if he has aligned his conscience. "They're my people. It has to be me."

"I may only be half wilder," I say, "but please don't feel like you're alone in this."

Galen grasps my hand. His strong, lean fingers squeeze mine as if he appreciates my sentiment. "When it begins," he says, "stay alert. The wilders will fight quick and dirty. They'll attack from all sides without any need to get close. Hand-to-hand combat is their weakness. While they're physically strong, their training and skill sets are all about their powers. We get close to them, we can take them out."

"How do you get close?"

"Speed. Luck. Strength. Then keep punching as hard as you can until they fall."

I take a deep breath to settle my rising dread. I realise I've been hoping words and logic will win the day. Will it really come to such brutality?

I swallow down the sour taste of fear.

Thank goodness for the fight training Havander gave me.

The councillors are waiting for us when we arrive at the clearing. Gathered in the centre of the ruined forest, they gleam ethereal, their lean forms clad in chain mail and water-wrought armour.

Neru, Cephos, Hestia, and Zephyrine—devils wearing the faces of angels—come to deliver what they believe to be righteous retribution.

We halt and our own defenders assemble at my back. Long, forked snake tongues whisper over their scaled lips. Dan and Dad, also in their serpent forms, flank me at each side.

In the silence that momentarily falls, the soft nicker of a horse betrays a force hidden in the forest beyond. I wonder if that is where Dacien is.

Neru takes a step forward, his ebony hair flowing like ink.

"Reeva," he says, surprise colouring his tone. "You've already gathered them for us?"

I straighten my shoulders. A beat of sweat trickles down my spine. I force strength into my words.

"The changers aren't here for your convenience, Councillor."

Neru's fingers flex. Barely concealed emotion—disappointment and frustration—crease his features. He gave me a chance, he saved my life and now I've turned on him.

"You've joined them," he says, more a statement than question.

"It was the right thing to do."

Neru's sapphire gaze rakes across the changers. "You know our laws and still you choose to hide behind a child. Changers—you have sealed her fate. Reeva's blood is on your hands."

"They asked for nothing. I made my own choice, Neru," I assert. "What happens next is on you and yours."

"What happens next?" laughs Zephyrine. "What happens next, child, is that you will die for your crimes and those you stand with will submit to new anklets, or perish with you."

Dan raises his head and chuckles, his tone slithery and serpentine. "We all stand together here. Rest assured, if you don't surrender today, release our kin and let us live free, it's you who'll perish."

Zephyrine scowls. "Your threats mean nothing to us. Changer freedom will never be given nor won."

"So you will continue to enslave us and encourage humanity's ignorance?" asks Dan. "Your arrogance is beyond comprehension."

"Our arrogance ensures the safety of this planet," roars Cephos.

Hestia places a slim-fingered hand on Cephos's arm. The earth councillor's cheeks bunch as he chews on words, unspoken.

"There is no arguing with inferior creatures," says Hestia. "We are done here. End them all and let us go home."

Her words are clothed in fire and forged with determination, but I recognise the fear behind them. Conversation is dangerous for her. Secrets could be revealed. She wants this day won quickly and without witnesses left, so her lies are kept covert. My own mother is still willing to kill to protect herself.

My hands and my chest tighten painfully. I take a

ragged breath and lift my chin. She is in my world now. A world where light reveals the lie. Let her face what she fears most.

"Ready to fight when you are, Mother Dear."

I barely recognise the malice in my own voice, but I do identify with the inherent cruelty in betraying her secret—of my wanting to sign her death warrant just as she had mine.

I guess I get that quality from my mother.

Hestia bunches her fists and her eyes thin to gleaming embers. She must recognise herself in me also.

The other councillors have registered what's been said. Neru watches Hestia, his demeanour calculating. Cephos watches her, uncertainty colouring his features.

"What is she talking about, Hestia?" asks Zephyrine in a hissing whisper. "Is this girl *your* child?"

"Don't be ridiculous!" snaps Hestia, sparks tripping between her fingers. "She lies to weaken our unity."

"But years ago … those months you were away …" mutters Cephos.

Hestia's slitted pupils contract. Before Cephos can finish his sentence, she builds a fire in her fist.

"Attack!" she screams.

Mounted wilders erupt from the undergrowth, colliding with the serpents poised to bite. I activate my shield, ignoring the sudden sting of pain, and encircle

Galen, Dan, and Dad within its perimeter. Battle cries and the sizzle of activated powers fill the clearing.

The first casualty is a young air woman. Her end is a scream and the gurgle of blood from a throat torn open by changer fangs. Her horse gallops off into the forest.

"Watch for the councillors," yells Galen, hefting his axe.

But Neru, Zephyrine, and Cephos are focused elsewhere. Wrestling alongside the mounted guard, their combined powers fill the air blistering off the armoured backs of the serpents. With fangs bared and venom dripping, the changers advance, determination steeling them against the wilder onslaught. Cephos growls and kneels, pressing his hands to the ground. The earth groans at his touch and heaves, fracturing open. Two serpents fall hissing into the ink-black cleft, lost to the darkness. Cephos closes it behind them.

"Let me out," growls Dan and I lower my shield for an instant. He slithers past me and launches for the earth councillor. Dan's muscled tail lashes out and encircles Cephos's armoured collar. The tall wilder's glowing hands clutch the coiled flesh strangling him. Neru and Zephyrine step in. Rain and turbulent air, wild as a storm, whip the glade. Dan's grip slips and he flies backwards. I brace myself, heels to earth, but other changers, further out, are torn from the ground— hurled and broken against the trees at the edge of the clearing.

Cephos rallies and attacks again. His magic carves out the back plate of Dan's armour, leaving a smoking hole behind. Dan roars in pain and rage, then slumps to the side, his coils falling lax. Dad reacts with a virulent hiss. With glittering fangs bared, he launches at Cephos, and locks his savage jaws onto the earth wilder's throat. Cephos cries out and his power flares then fades. He crumbles to the ground next to Dan, eyes emptied of life, blood and violet-coloured changer venom staining his chest. My stomach surges, horrified, as he slumps to stillness.

I didn't think Dad had it in him to kill ...

I stumble back as Dan struggles to move. Finally he gathers his coils and lengthens his neck to rise. The injured changer shakes his head and then strikes out and trips Zephyrine as she glides past, her power levelled towards Dad.

She recovers with a flip, aged but still agile. Then, fierce and skilled, she turns to Dan, hair wild like serpents and fists holding typhoons.

But she has forgotten my father. She is no match for him, no match for the rage of Emmett Castor.

And in a slick of blood and cry of pain, she falls to her death beside her colleague.

To my left, there's movement. I glance across. With Cephos and Zephyrine both dead, Neru flees for the cover of the forest.

And Hestia comes for me, a reptilian coldness held in the press of her lips. Her fingers drip with magic—a rain of embers trailed by streamers of smoke. I tremble with the effort of sustaining my power. Pain lances through my shoulder and into my spine.

"I can't hold the shield any more," I sob.

Galen nods. His white-knuckled grip shifts on his axe's handle.

"Let it go," he says.

My magic flickers again and the barrier drops.

My arm throbs, the ache all encompassing and resolute. I blink away dots that gather at the edges of my vision. I've overexerted myself but regret nothing. Trembling, fatigued, I somehow find the strength to assume the fighting stance Havander taught me.

"You're pathetic," snarls Hestia, her words wielded as weapons. "Weak, just like your father." She stops ten paces away, her unmarked chain mail clinking. "And is that you there, Galen Earthborn, protecting her? How far you have fallen. Tell me, do you enjoy being human? I honestly thought it would have killed you by now."

"You've always been *such* a bitch, Hestia," says Galen.

"You aren't the first to say so," she replies.

My mother thrusts her fist forward. Her power crackles through the air, blistering hot—deadly. Heat floods outwards in a wave. The shrubs at the edge of the clearing smoulder.

Galen's axe head draws the brunt of Hestia's assault. Still gripping the handle, he's thrown backwards, limbs splayed. He lands and doesn't move.

"Galen!" I leap forward, but a whip-like crack of Hestia's power stops me.

My mother grins, triumphant. "He deserves to die," she says.

And with those words, I find the anger Dad told me to look for. I'm sick of losing friends, of seeing good people get hurt. Adrenaline slices through me. The rage balled in my gut grows and underpins the structure of my power. My scar splits. I sob as both blood and magic pour from the wound.

Strands of scarlet twist through with the silver-white light—my human and wilder DNA combining with natural magic to become something new—something hybrid. Hestia's face falls as the alien power coils around my wrist, rising like a whirlwind.

"Stop it!" she screams. "It's blasphemy!"

I clench my fist. The magic solidifies and an ice spear forms in my hand—clear with a core of scarlet blood.

Finally, the weapon I've always failed to make.

With a roar, I aim for Hestia's heart. It feels right. It feels justified—

But then my brother steps in between us.

CHAPTER TWENTY-TWO

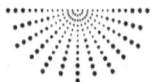

"Don't do it, Reeva."

I hadn't seen Dacien during the fighting, but the dirt and blood smearing his face tells me he was in the thick of it. Now he holds out both hands, magic quelled. His plea comes from the heart, not a threat or a demand. He wants to protect his mother.

Hestia, on the other hand, uses her son as a shield. She huddles behind him, clutching Dacien's shoulder in a white-knuckled grip. My command of hybrid abilities has obviously rattled her.

Hell, somewhere deep inside, I'm rattled too.

Around us the battle continues—a cacophony of snarls and cries—but nothing matters except my burning desire to end this.

My ice spear trembles like it has a heartbeat. It's mirroring my own pulse.

"I'm sorry I didn't believe you," continues Dacien, his unblinking gaze pinned to mine. "But I do now."

"Why?" I ask.

"She admitted it. She's your mother. We are … siblings."

Too late.

I heft the spear. "Get out of the way, Dacien. I don't want to hurt you."

"But I helped when you needed it," he says. "I taught you how to use your magic. You owe me this."

"I owe you nothing. It was always Havander who helped me. He lost his *life* helping me."

Dacien's face pales.

"That's right," I say, bitterly. "He didn't make it."

My father looking tired, but resolute, approaches. Returned to his human form, his face is streaked with dirt and ash. He glances at my brother and then away, features unreadable.

"Let it go, Reeva," he says. "If you hurt Hestia, you'll never forgive yourself."

"I think I will," I say.

"No," says Dad. "You're more human than wilder. Where she feels nothing, you feel everything twice as hard. You always have."

I swallow. "I hate her."

Dad nods. "I know, but don't let it consume you."

I lower the spear. Dacien shuffles nervously on his feet. I remind myself he isn't all that old. He's younger than me after all and, to be honest, it's not him I despise.

"Take *her*," I say, to my brother, "in return for the liberation of *all* changers."

"Never!" Hestia's cry slices the air like a knife. She strikes out, her arm circling Dacien's neck and pulling him backwards. Caught unawares, he cries out and struggles as she clutches him to her chest.

"What are you doing, Mother?"

Wordless, Hestia jabs her free arm up. A lasso of fire scorches from her fist, lassoing Emmett around his shoulders. He cries out as he is dragged struggling into her grasp also.

"You think you've won?" she snarls at me.

Dad tries to change shape but with his powers newly-made and caged by Hestia's fire, he panics and fails. His form resolves back into human. "You're a bloody coward, Hestia!" he growls.

Hestia wrestles him into submission and wrenches her hand across his mouth. "Act the good slave, Emmett," she sneers, "and be quiet."

Dad struggles on silently, but Hestia is too strong.

I lift my spear again. Its power throbs through my blood, the strength of it causing a dull ache behind my eyes. "Let them go or I'll kill you."

Hestia grins. "And which one of these will you sacrifice to get to me? Which one, Reeva? Your father or your brother?"

"Mother?" croaks Dacien. His own power sparks and sputters around his fists, but never fully resolves. Something about Hestia's magic is blocking his.

Hestia shakes her son. "Shut up."

My brother stills, his features turned to granite. But the heartache of her betrayal is clear in the set of his jaw.

I juggle the spear in my grasp, suddenly uncertain.

Dad or Dacien?

Father or brother?

Both are family.

"I'm sorry, Dacien," I whisper, letting loyalty to my father hold sway.

My brother closes his eyes.

Forgive me.

I throw the spear true. The ice sings as it flies, it punctures Dacien's shoulder, continuing through to skewer Hestia.

Dacien grunts in pain. My mother screams and her grip on Dad falters. She shoves her son away from her, slithering off the ice. Dacien falls to his knees, bloodied.

Dad finally shapeshifts, his flesh blurring from human to snake. He coils his serpentine tail around Hestia, pulling her to the ground under the weight of his coils. She screeches and her fire blisters along his scales, smoking ruts left in their wake. But Dad has waited too long for this moment. He squeezes her and finally Hestia surrenders, full of rage, but impotent.

"You're done," says my father.

One more thrash against her bonds and the Hestia stops. A type of quiet descends, punctuated only by soft voices and forest sounds. No more battle cries or the sizzle of magic.

It's then I realise the skirmish has ended and we have won. A small crowd of wilders stand huddled together at the edge of the clearing, guarded by a few of the changer fighters, now in their natural, humanoid forms. Horses, some with bloodstained saddles and others with reins trailing, pick their way across the open space, at a loss of where to go.

The clearing is littered with corpses. The remaining changers move amongst them, arranging them into rows. Zephyrine and Cephos are set slightly apart from the other dead—their status, even in death, being respected by the changers. Close by, Neru barely clings to life, a pallid hand pressed to a deep wound in his stomach. Galen lies unconscious next to him. Dan holds the ex-wilder's head in his lap.

"Rigeander," I call and from the trees the old changer appears, covered in blood, but looking a hundred years younger than he did. He wears freedom well. "Help Dad secure Hestia and if you don't mind, please heal both her and my brother."

"For you, Reeva, gladly," he replies, making his way over.

I glance at Dacien. He's on his knees, still bleeding, head bent to his chest. He defiantly ignores me. I want to make things good with him, but recognise that now is not the time. Instead, I retrieve my ice spear from the ground, its solid, cold weight feeling good in my hand.

"Stay here," I say to him. "I'll be back in a minute."

Neru, his teeth bloodied, tries to smile as I approach, but only manages a cough. It doesn't take a doctor to see he is dying.

"I underestimated you," he whispers.

"You did," I reply.

He motions towards Hestia with his free hand. "It would be dangerous to leave her as the sole living council member."

"Why do you think we'd let her keep her station?"

"You'll grant her freedom because you need her. There are sacred rituals to be honoured when inducting new councillors. When I'm gone, she's the only one left with the knowledge and she will choose those loyal only to her."

I don't trust Neru, but I know he's right.

"What will you give us for your life?"

A quick intake of breath and fresh blood leaks past Neru's fingers. "The changers."

"They already have their freedom."

"No. I mean … I'll return to them their seat on the council—as equals."

I recall the empty throne in the citadel.

Dan, still sitting by Galen, straightens. I can almost taste his desperate desire—he'd willingly bear the scar of healing Neru for such a prize.

"How can I be sure you'd do it?" I ask.

Neru coughs again and slumps back. His hand slips from his stomach. The wound is deep. He's weakening.

"I'll wear an anklet," he murmurs, pulling off his blood-slick bracelet and handing it to me. "One controlled by someone of your choosing. Make Hestia wear one too. Your father might like the job of managing her."

"You knew about them then—about me?"

"I knew your mother's secret. I kept it in case I needed to use it against her."

I roll back on my heels, considering his offer. It's a fair deal. I gesture and Dan moves to Neru's side. With the injury so dire, the changer calls three of his people over and together they circle the stricken wilder. Their fingertips illuminate and together they press them to Neru's wound. Minutes pass and his flesh slowly stitches together, the healing circle's magic doing its work. Dan finally nods at me.

The water wilder will live.

And the changers are finally free.

CHAPTER TWENTY-THREE

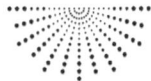

Dusk has fallen and the spilled blood has seeped away into the earth. The dead have been sung into trees and the remaining wilders, led by Neru, have returned to The Styx. The horses, all re-captured, are safely stabled at the Anderson farm.

Only my mother and brother left to deal with.

"Neru doesn't speak for me," hisses Hestia. "I'll make no bargain that forces me to wear an anklet."

My mother stands with Dacien by the Elder Tree. Although healed, they both look battle-worn, their armour stained with blood.

Rigeander holds the anklet in his determined hand. "Neru already got his. It's your turn now, Councillor. The anklet or prison? And that's pretty fair either way. Your own laws would have called for worse considering what you've done."

"You know nothing," says Hestia, fists balled at her sides.

"Please, Mother," says Dacien, his tone clipped, "our people need you."

He hasn't looked at or spoken to me. I try to catch his eye again, but he avoids it. I feel sorry for my brother. He didn't ask for any of this.

Hestia turns on him. "Where is the benefit in being stunted?" she screeches. "How can I be of any use with *changers* governing my powers? I will not yield control."

"Do it or I'll bloody strap that anklet on you myself," says Dad, striding up.

"You always were an animal, Emmett," snarls Hestia.

He chuckles. "Better an animal than slave to your bloodbind."

"I did it to protect my people."

"Bullshit. You did it for yourself."

"Enough," says Rigeander, rattling the anklet. "Make your choice, Councillor."

Hestia smiles, her white teeth gleaming. "I choose … autonomy."

She shoves against Rigeander. He stumbles back and the anklet flies from his hand, landing in a nearby clump of ferns. Dad snatches at Hestia but misses. She doesn't hesitate. Turning, she flees into the forest, red hair flying behind her like scraps of broken sunset against the evening shadows.

"Mother!" calls Dacien.

He races past the Elder Tree and stops, peering into the night. Only the lonely hoot of a Masked Owl filters through the bush. Hestia is gone. My brother's shoulders straighten. He turns, seemingly emotionless. But I'm not fooled. His eyes give his heart away—that turbulent blue they turn when he tries to hide his feelings.

The muscles in his cheeks work. "With your permission," he says, "I'll return home."

Rigeander nods. With the touch of his hand, the portal opens and my brother steps away without a backward glance.

My heart clenches around the words I would've liked to say to him. To say I'm sorry. To say he isn't alone, and that I wish things could have been different.

My father rubs a hand across his mouth. "Give him time, Reeva," he says. "The boy has a lot to process. After a bit though, he might miss having family. I'll let him know that you're about if he wants to reach out."

"What do you mean you'll let him know?"

Dad smiles. "You've looked after me long enough. It's time you took your own path—headed back to university, maybe. And I'll stick around here, look after the farm and keep an eye on this crowd." He winks. "Someone needs to make sure Dan doesn't get a big head now that he's been made a high and mighty councillor."

"Councillor Danander has a ring to it."

"It's better than Dan Anderson isn't it?" says Dad.

"Definitely. But what about Hestia? She's still out there."

Dad looks away into the gloom. The tiny noises of the night surround us as the temperature falls closer towards freezing.

I hug my arms around myself.

"She is," says Dad, finally. "But your mother is alone.

If she stays away too long, she'll become human like Galen. She won't want that. We'll hear from her again soon enough and we can negotiate with her then."

"Negotiate?"

"Yep. You can read that as 'slap an anklet on her'."

"Gotcha."

Dad chuckles and drapes his arm around my neck. "I'm tired," he says. "Let's head home and grab a cup of tea."

"You want tea?" I ask, surprised.

"Yeah," says Dad with a sniff. "Go figure, but apparently alcohol is poisonous to changers. About bloody right when it comes to me and my luck."

CHAPTER TWENTY-FOUR

Only two weeks have passed, but it feels like a lifetime.

The grey sky huddles low, but is not yet ready to break. A breeze wraps chilly around my legs, seeping in through my jeans and across the back of my neck. But for once, I don't mind the cold. My suitcase sits on the bench beside me. I'm anxious and nervous, but fear is not going to stop me.

I'm free and have a future to claim.

I check my watch. It's nine o'clock in the morning. Up the road, the Maydena fish and chip shop is just opening and the carpark to the IGA has three cars parked in it. That's almost flat-out-full for this town. The bus I'm waiting for to take me to Hobart and a new term at university, however is still nowhere to be seen. I lean back against the bench, cross my arms over my chest and close my eyes.

"Can I join you?"

I recognise the smell of Galen's aftershave. I look up

and smile. He's dressed in his police uniform, two steaming cups of coffee in hand.

"What, no donuts?" I ask.

Galen chuckles and sits next to me. The grim day suddenly seems all the cheerier.

"Emmett rang," he says. "He said you were being stubborn and sneaking off without saying goodbye to anyone. He asked me to come and sit with you."

"Thanks." I accept the offered coffee and take a sip. The chocolate-laced froth fills my mouth and slides down my throat warming me from the inside. "I just wanted to show him that I'm okay to do this myself. Besides, he's busy in The Styx helping rebuild Ashnah Keep. They've torn down the prison, you know, and are creating a new village. He's constantly fighting with Dan though."

Galen laughs. "No surprise there. But even though he's busy, he's your dad too. He wants to look out for you if he can."

"It's nice to be looked out for, for once," I say.

Galen takes a mouthful of coffee. He watches the IGA carpark and an old woman pushing a trolley towards her vehicle. "So, it's now off to university again?"

"Yep. Returning to finish a Bachelor Degree in Environmental Studies," I say. "Then I might do as Neru suggested. It wasn't such a bad idea. I can be a mouthpiece to promote the wilder message for conservation."

"Sounds like a plan," says Galen. He takes another sip of coffee. "It's funny, isn't it, that you chose to study that in the first instance? You wanted to help the planet even before you knew what you were."

"I hadn't thought of it like that before. But maybe it's not surprising, given we live in a place like Tasmania."

"One of the last, true wild places."

Silence follows and an awkward sense of words, unspoken, hangs between us.

"Hey," says Galen, hesitantly. "Can I ask you something?"

"Sure."

"What would you say if I suggested I might miss you when you leave?"

My heart skitters sideways. I look at my cup, not trusting he won't see what I'm really thinking.

I try to sound casual. "Well, I'd say, there are plenty of girls around town who'll do their best to make sure you won't."

"But can *any* of them make armour out of water?" he asks with a chuckle.

I rub my scar, sensing the power flowing just beneath it.

"Probably not," I say, and then run out of words.

The coach swings into view. The bright red paint-work is a splash of colour against the snaking bitumen. Its engine roars smoothly and then slows as the driver changes gears. I flag him. The indicator light goes on.

"Let me help with your bag," says Galen, setting his coffee down on the bench.

He carries my luggage to the curb as I adjust my satchel over my shoulder. My hands tremble with uncertainty. Do I tell him how I really feel or just stick with my plan and go?

I take a breath and follow him. The bus eases to a stop and the side storage panel opens. The driver exits and places my suitcase inside.

I hate goodbyes. I turn to Galen and hug him. He returns it, his arms a warm circle around my shoulders.

"Catch you later, Constable Mayer," I say.

"I hope so," he replies.

"And thanks for everything."

"You're welcome," he says.

I step away and risk looking Galen in the eye. Is it my nervousness or the logical part of my brain telling me to leave it here with him, like this? I remind myself that I've grown. I'm powerful. I don't need to shrink away from the world anymore.

My feelings are valid and I should say what I want.

"Will you come visit me in Hobart?" I blurt out.

"So you're saying you *will* miss me?"

"Yeah. I guess. A little."

He smiles, small and tight. "Why am I not feeling convinced?"

I breathe out. He isn't making this easy for me.

"Fine. I'll miss you this much."

My heart hammers unevenly as I place both hands on his cheeks and pull him close. His lips are soft and warm against mine. Then all my awkwardness and uncertainty falls away when he smiles against my mouth and tugs me closer, returning a kiss filled with promise.

Behind me, the bus driver yells from his seat. "Let's go, I'm on a schedule here!"

Breaking away is like coming up for air. "See you soon?" I whisper.

"Looking forward to it," he says, eyes dancing.

I turn and grasp the rail, heart brimming. This is it. I take the three steps leading into the bus—three small steps that are the first to this future of my own choosing.

ACKNOWLEDGEMENTS

My sincere thanks go to Angela Slatter who worked with me on the first drafts of this novella. I couldn't have written this book without your help. Thank you to Selina Shapland for her thoughtful coaching. Thanks also to Lauren Elise Daniels and Geneve Flynn, for their endless support. Thanks to Gina Pinto and Jan-Andrew Henderson for their keen eyes, kindness and generosity in looking over the final manuscript.

To Aiki Flinthart. I promised you I would finish this book. I hope I have made you proud.

To the Queensland Writers Centre, thank you for selecting me as the recipient of the 2021 Flinthart Writing Residency. This book would not exist without your exceptional and ongoing support. I am forever grateful.

And finally, as always, my family. Thank you for your endless love and support. You are my everything.

ABOUT THE AUTHOR

Pamela Jeffs is an Australian speculative fiction author with a background in Interior Architecture and Design. She has published six short story collections and has 90+ short stories featured in various national and international publications. Pamela's work has received recognition in the Australian Aurealis Awards having won the 2023 Horror Short Story Category and has also shortlisted eleven other times in previous years. She has also shortlisted for multiple other awards including, to date, three Ditmar Awards and two Australasian Shadow Awards.

Wilder is her first novella, made possible by the Queensland Writers Centre and the Flinthart Writing Residency programme.

To discover more books by Pamela Jeffs, visit and subscribe at:

www.pamelajeffs.com
Facebook: @pamelajeffsauthor
Twitter: @Pamela_Jeffs
Instagram: @pamela_jeffs
Bluesky: @pamelajeffs.bsky.social